A WAY TO BE HAPPY

A WAY TO BE HAPPY

STORIES

CAROLINE ADDERSON

BIBLIOASIS * WINDSOR, ONTARIO

FIRST EDITION
10 9 8 7 6 5 4 3 2 1

Library and Archives Canada Cataloguing in Publication
Title: A way to be happy : stories / Caroline Adderson.
Names: Adderson, Caroline, 1963- author.
Identifiers: Canadiana (print) 20240370724 | Canadiana (ebook)
20240370732 ISBN 9781771966221 (softcover) | ISBN 9781771966238
(EPUB)
Subjects: LCGFT: Short stories.
Classification: LCC PS8551.D3267 W39 2024 | DDC jC813/.54—dc23

Edited by Daniel Wells
Copyedited by Chandra Wohleber
Designed and typeset by Vanessa Stauffer

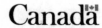 

Published with the generous assistance of the Canada Council for the Arts,
which last year invested $153 million to bring the arts to Canadians through-
out the country, and the financial support of the Government of Canada. Biblioasis also acknowledges the support of the Ontario Arts Council (OAC), an
agency of the Government of Ontario, which last year funded 1,709 individual
artists and 1,078 organizations in 204 communities across Ontario, for a total
of $52.1 million, and the contribution of the Government of Ontario through
the Ontario Book Publishing Tax Credit and Ontario Creates.

The writing of this book was supported by grants from the British Columbia
Arts Council and the Canada Council for the Arts.

PRINTED AND BOUND IN CANADA

For John,

We meet again . . .

Astrov: People a hundred years or two hundred years from now, who despise us for having lived such stupid and tasteless lives—perhaps they'll find a way to be happy...As for us...There's only one hope for you and me...The hope that when we're asleep in our graves, visions might visit us—perhaps even pleasant ones.

ANTON CHEKHOV,
Uncle Vanya

CONTENTS

ALL OUR AULD
ACQUAINTANCES ARE GONE

ONLY ABOUT HALF the apartments were lit and fewer had Christmas lights, just like the last building. They must have walked around the block and ended up back at the same glassy, germless place. Even the Christmas tree in the white marble lobby was a twin, down to the ornaments.

She asked Cory, "Weren't we just here?"

He'd found cigarettes and a lighter in the coat pocket. When he answered smoke hung on his words, or the cold wrote them in the air.

"That was back by where we parked. Same builder probably. Half these condos are empty. They're investments."

He'd worked in construction, so she believed him, just like she believed him when he'd said one party. Somebody had told him about it and she went along. Then, when they were leaving, walking all natural down the hall to the elevator in their new coats and shoes, they passed an open door where another party was happening. The loud music sucked Cory in.

Nobody spoke to her at the first party, but at the second this dude with sideburns came over and asked, "And what are you going to do to make your pretty little life sparkle in 2020?"

Now here they were when they should have been driving, but Cory was on a roll, going for three times lucky, whatever that meant. She'd never known it even once. An ache kicked her in different places. Behind one eye.

"What time is it?" she asked.

He hiked the coat up at the back to get at his phone. "Eleven sixteen."

"I'm feeling like Cinderella here."

"I know."

"So let's go. We're good now."

"How're those shoes?"

She looked down at them. They'd picked a shadow to wait in, a spot between the streetlight and the light pouring out of the glassed-in lobby. Darkness drained the crayon colour from the shoes. Green with purple piping, buckles.

"I feel stupid."

"Be careful how you walk. Don't do that thing."

"What thing?"

"Half the time you look about to fall over."

This made her want to sit down. She went over to the planter and sank her ass onto the cold cement. She'd left the last place with one of those shiny gift bags with string handles. It clinked when she set it on the ground.

"Feel this." Cory held out his arm. "It's cashmere."

Meaning expensive. It suited him with his new haircut. The first few days without his dirty yellow dreads, she'd kept forgetting. She'd be waiting some place and this dude with a fade would come along. He'd only turn into Cory when he smiled.

Or Kayla would nudge her. Kayla always knew him right away, would twist her hair around one finger and sigh.

Two men walked past, one in a ski jacket, the other an overcoat, tall and short. Then a car drove by so slowly it was impossible not to feel watched. Looking for parking, it turned out. Cold in the thin raincoat, she curled over and hugged herself. Her gaze met the wine. At least she'd thought it was wine when she grabbed the bag off the table, but only now did she reach inside.

Wine. There was a card too, which she drew out and opened. An angel on one knee, like it was proposing. She tossed it into the planter behind her just as her leg spasmed.

"Cramp?" he asked.

She nodded, one foot off the ground, leg stretched out like she was admiring the gay-ass shoe. "You?"

"I'm fine. I'm pumped."

The fingers of pain slowly released. *I'm not doing this*. She opened her mouth to say it, but just then a couple turned off the sidewalk and started walking toward them. Cory nodded as they passed.

He switched to his animal mode then, eyes focused on some point in the distance, though he wasn't seeing anything. He was listening to the beeping as the couple punched a number into the building's intercom, then its amplified ringing. At precisely the right moment he made a dart of the cigarette and headed for the door. She picked up the wine and followed, lurching on the shoes.

The door buzzed. The dude, Indian or something, held it open for his white girlfriend. Cory came up fast behind them. "Going to the party?"

Dude hesitated, still holding the door. He had a goatee and a diamond stud in one ear. "Joe and Perry's?"

"Yeah." Cory smiled without the missing tooth. Farther back in his mouth, it only showed when he smiled for real. "But we can get buzzed in, no problem. We were just having a smoke before going up."

Dude flicked his eyes over them, stopping on the gift bag hanging on her arm. His girlfriend was already in the lobby, their own wine jutting from her oversized handbag, just the neck of it, a twist of brown paper. Shrugging, he let go of the door.

Cory caught it and kept two steps behind. She tripped along after them, heart having a fit now that they were inside.

At the elevator Cory lunged for the Up button. That way Dude would press the button for the floor. At least that was what happened last time. While they waited, they looked in four directions—at the white-baubled tree in the corner, the lobby's white walls screaming for a spray can, the numbers lighting up then dying with the elevator's descent. The girlfriend inspected her perfect nails.

The elevator came and they stepped inside. Sure enough, Dude punched twenty-four. She kept her eyes on the floor numbers counting up now. The weightless sensation should have cancelled out the dread. Dude's spicy aftershave didn't help. She put her hand on her stomach, feeling through the coat for the rectangular comfort of her phone.

At floor twelve Dude broke the silence. "So are you a lawyer too?"

His girlfriend nudged him. She had long, stiff blond hair and makeup that looked like it might flake off.

"Oh, right. That's an inappropriate question. What can I ask him, hon?"

"For one, you could have asked if *she* was a lawyer."

An exhalation of scorn escaped her, though no one seemed to hear it.

Cory said, "Ask my favourite cereal then."

"No. Let me guess it. You're a muesli man, am I right?"

The woman rolled her eyes. "I'm Michelle. He's Raj." She gave him a jab, which he pretended hurt.

"I'm Scott," Cory said.

She blanked on the name they'd decided for her this time. Different name, different coat, different shoes, different hair. Different people in the security video in the identical lobbies. But the name was gone, like Kayla. Where was she? Muesli was porridge, sort of. Breakfast was a half-finished Starbucks drink fished out of the trash. Or did he have muesli this morning at his mom's?

They were looking at her, waiting.

"I'm Angel." It just popped into her head.

Cory stiffened beside her.

"I love your shoes," Michelle said. "Are they Fluevogs?"

The elevator pinged and opened. Raj stepped out first. "See, I would find that an inappropriate question. What if she got them at Walmart?"

Michelle shook her head. "I don't think so."

"What if I stole them?" she said, and they all laughed.

The four of them headed down the hall, Cory squeezing her shoulder, holding her back. *WTF?* it meant. They could hear the party up ahead, the throb of music, shout-talking. A tingling broke out across her face. She lifted her shoulder and tried to shake Cory off.

They both started to slow as they neared the party. The smaller gestures, like pressing the Up button first, like going ahead as if they knew the way—they'd talked about this. It bolstered their cred. But now Cory was squeezing. *Don't act like a nutcase, babe.* If they'd been walking in front they would have blown it because Raj and Michelle sailed right past the party door. So they did too.

Cory loosened his grip. Patted her back.

"We can drop in there if Joe's sucks," Raj said.

"This is our third party. We aren't staying long." She said it to Cory.

"Popular," Raj said. "It's our first."

"We had dinner with my mom," Michelle explained.

Joe and Perry's was just two doors along, same side. Raj knocked pointlessly before opening the door and nearly hitting somebody standing just inside. Techno music poured out. He and Michelle went in sideways.

Now she said it, what she'd wanted to tell Cory out front. "I can't. Give me some money."

"In and out, like you said."

"I mean *at all.* I can't do *any* of it. I don't *want to.*"

Cory took her face in his hands—clean now, even his nails—but still textured from the street. Forehead pressed against hers, eyes an inch away, he drove his resolve right into her. "Yes, you can... Angel."

Hand on her back, he guided her inside.

Michelle had taken off her coat, exposing a meaty nylon bulge of thigh between boot tops and skirt. She was staring at the footwear piled around the door.

"Do we have to take off our shoes? It ruins your outfit."

"I'm having sock insecurity," Raj said.

Michelle said to her, "You're not taking yours off, are you?"

She pointed to the people lingering at the end of the hall. Some were wearing shoes. Michelle smiled and, passing Raj her coat, strode off in her boots. Raj frowned at the hooks that lined the wall, already layered with coats. No vacancy in the closet either.

A woman in a fringed wrap stepped out of the room off the hall. "They're putting them on the bed now," she said. Raj ducked in with their coats, then out again empty-handed. With a wave to them, he went after Michelle, disappearing into the crowded main room.

She took off the raincoat. Under it, a short black dress with complicated sleeves, hardly sleeves at all, sheer nylon stitched to the thicker fabric of the dress. Below the elbow, they flared. If she held her arms out at her sides that part of the sleeve hung down like wings. She'd got it for the kangaroo pocket, to carry her phone. Boxing Week at Winners. The harried clerks, past the point of caring, only counted the hangers before handing over the numbered plastic disc, not the clothes actually on the hangers. Anybody can take off a security tag with a hair elastic. Kayla had taught her. Three Kaylas in the wings of the change room mirror, ball cap and bra, ink flowers twining up her arms. They'd braided friendship bracelets for each other like they were eight or something. Their names made them sound like sisters. She wound the elastic around the tag the way Kayla showed her. It popped right off and Kayla smiled her own broken smile.

Cory was having trouble giving up his coat. Before handing it over, he held it by the collar and brushed at some unseeable speck. He showed her the label sewn inside. "See? Cashmere." Draping it across her waiting arms, he said, "Goodbye."

"I'll be fast," she said. "Don't go away."

"I'm talking to the coat."

She stepped into the room, closing the door just enough

that the music receded to a pulse. All the way would look suspicious, though she was less nervous about getting caught now than anxious to get it done. The only light was a lamp on the bedside table draped with some kind of cloth, which dimmed the room even more. Gradually, she made out a pile of coats on the bed, tossed theirs into it, then craned to see into the space next to the wall where the purses were stashed. She added the bag with the wine.

The first curdling wave hit her then. She shut her eyes and swayed, hand pressing her phone, on fire and drenched at the same time. A blunt, bitter stab against the back of her throat— just a hint of what was coming. All of this was pointless. No way could she do it. Maybe Cory could. He hadn't been around that long. Also, something was waiting for him on the other side, in that other life where she wasn't welcome. She'd gone and seen it that afternoon, taken the SkyTrain all the way out in her winged dress, soared over the different-coloured roofs and shiny toy cars parked along the streets. His mother said he could move back in if he cleaned up. But not her. He'd been there two nights, had snuck her in so they could get ready for tonight.

"Holy, look at you," he'd said.

His mother's heavy tread crossed the low ceiling. Just a shitty bungalow with a basement suite that stank of bleach. But compared to the underpass? Or the tarp they'd rigged up over two carts until one of them got jacked? Last night, while Cory slept in his boyhood home, she went off with some dude who said they could crash where they impounded the cars. In the morning, she woke alone to crows croaking and rattling, condensation all over the windows, a silver nest made of her breath. Her jeans tossed onto the hood of the car, soaked with rain. She couldn't remember a thing about how they got there. She missed Kayla so bad then.

The wave passed. She rubbed her arms through the sleeves. Something prickled the back of her neck. An instinct, or some higher numbered sense. Eyes boring into her. She thought of Kayla's, the way they rolled back to show the red stitching of veins. Kayla splayed out on the ground, her cap three feet away. *But where did they take her?* she'd asked Cory. Where do you go after that?

Cory didn't know. All he'd said was *We're getting out of here.*

Somebody was in the room. She swung round. A bulky shape filled the chair in the corner.

"God! You scared me!"

It was a woman, half whispering. "Sorry."

"I was just wondering if it was safe to leave my purse."

Why had she made an excuse before she was accused of anything? She could have told the truth, that she'd stood there so long because she felt sick. But she was out of the habit. True things sounded like lies. She didn't even have a purse.

Again that hushed voice. "Stick it under there." The woman pointed at something with her stockinged foot.

She came closer. On the other side of the bed was a portable crib. She looked directly at the woman, first at her face in the shadows—dark hair, long nose. Then her bulkiness transformed to include the blanket draped over her shoulder and around the baby in her arms, the little toque perched on its head the only visible part of it.

Who would bring a baby to a loud party? It didn't seem that different from pushing a stroller down the alley looking to score—something she disapproved of too, though it was better than being passed from one non-mother to the next with your whole life stuffed in a garbage bag.

"I'll just stick it in my coat," she said, taking a step back.

She flitted her eyes around the room, trying to think of something normal to say before getting away. It didn't seem that dark now. Curtains, furniture—all revealed. The bass in the music made the picture above the woman's head vibrate against the wall like nervous teeth. She felt so bad for the baby.

"How old?"

"Three months," the woman said. "Which is about the last time I slept. He has no trouble sleeping of course. Unless I do. Then he immediately wakes up. They're funny things."

A bell tinkled in her pocket. She took the phone out and gestured toward the door with it.

The woman said, "Would you do me a favour? Bring me something to eat? I sent my husband, but he's gone AWOL."

"Sure."

"Thanks!"

She stepped into the hall. Cory had already hung up but was texting now.

How's it going

Somebody's in ther wher r u

Balcony

He was supposed to be watching out for her. She thumbed in *??? Let's go*

1 sec

Water trickled out of her nose. She pressed it with the back of her hand. Cory had the money and the cards. Otherwise she'd leave right now.

Another cramp. She braced against the wall to stretch it out. The coats hung there two or three deep, pockets begging to be searched. But there were people steps away at the end of the hall. They'd only have to turn their heads.

She tested the leg then walked straight into the party in the teetering way Cory hated.

There was a fireplace at one end of the room, an open kitchen at the other. Square furniture that nobody sat on. People stood in pairs or tight groups, elbow to elbow, talking loudly over the music. She cut through their groupings. Nobody looked at her.

A long table of food. She lifted the tongs and started loading a plate for the woman with the baby, thinking of cardboard. Cardboard flattened on the sidewalk. A smorgasbord of things you can eat mixed up with things you can't. Jars of No Name p.b., mission sandwiches, binned and stolen crap. Broken phones, granola bars, Percocet. She piled cubes and rolls on the plate. What half of it was, she didn't know. It looked like it would come back up whole.

Beyond the glass wall was a balcony almost as large as the inside space, and as crowded. Finally, she spotted him. With his bony face, he looked like a fake-junkie model in his new mother-bought clothes. He was talking to a man in a suit with a shaved head, touching his arm, for sure calling him *Bro*. It bugged her when he did that. Why? He *was* a brother. He came from an actual family. He could go live in Mommy's basement, *but not her*.

Those condemning footfalls.

She'd hardly lured Cory. They'd met downtown with Dani and that girl with the birthmark, and Kayla. Until Cory, she and Kayla shared everything. She'd worn her friendship bracelet, just a grubby string now, until tonight. Cory used scissors to cut it off. He threw it in the garbage. Another guy had hung with them too, an older Spanish dude who tried to teach them to trill their tongues and made them laugh their heads off. He was probably dead, like Kayla and the birthmark girl.

She pressed her open palm against the window, willing him to turn around. *Let's go.* Her own reflection superimposed on his, making one person. Like her and Kayla.

Turn around. Turn around.

Maybe thoughts couldn't pass through glass.

She stepped out the sliding door. It was much colder here, but not as loud. She balanced the plate on the railing, took out her phone: 11:34. She'd give him two minutes to come over. Or text.

Before her—silver towers and golden streets, a glitter-dusted far shore. The central darkness she knew to be water. It was dotted with lights from the tankers at anchor. Earlier that night, there'd been stars, but it had clouded over, erasing the mountains.

Somebody was smoking weed. With the first skunky whiff, she felt plucked in different parts of her body. Pinched. A thousand tiny hooks piercing her skin. She checked her phone.

This time when she lifted her eyes, she could tell clouds from sky. The city lit them from below. One looked like some-body floating face down in water, except her hair didn't spread but dangled like black stringy tentacles of a jellyfish. Streaks of rain probably. How many floors up were they? The building was lifting her higher. Every darkened window in it, and in every building—blackness. Black as that beautiful moment before you open your eyes to the paramedic staring down. He's shouting your name because he knows you from before. He knows your name. You don't know his, but you recognize him by how his face glows with blue-eyed joy.

The needle is in your thigh. Then you woof.

And still Cory didn't text or see her. He was somewhere on the other side of the balcony having a ball.

She almost forgot the plate of food. She picked it up and headed back inside.

THE BABY WAS hunched on the woman's shoulder now. All she could see of him was his back and the little toque of T-shirt material knotted at the top. Why did she think it was a boy? Had she said? No, the toque was blue.

She tried not to look at him. He was so small he made her feel like crying, which was a symptom too. Or maybe a memory. Yet there was nothing there, just the garbage bag and the things she was loading in it. Clothes. A Barbie. What did it say about you if the things you were allowed to love were packed up like trash? After so many moves, you just leave everything and go.

"Thanks," the woman said. She patted the dresser for her to set down the plate. "I'm starving."

She could grab any old purse now and go.

"Want to hold him?"

She jerked back, which made the woman laugh.

"I didn't use to like them either, believe it or not." She reached for one of the curls on the plate and let it unfurl into her mouth. Ham, it looked like. Her hand covered her chewing. "I didn't realize there'd be so many people here. Now I don't want to leave him. He's just about asleep. Then I'll go get his dad."

She just stood there, arms limp, scalp prickling, desperate now to scratch. The baby drowsed like a baby.

"I'm Miranda, by the way. Joe's sister."

"I'm Angel."

Oh, it was an angel that she'd seen from the balcony. She thought it might have been Kayla.

"That's such a pretty name. Do you have a resolution?"

She gave in and grated her scalp with her nails. "What?"

"A New Year's resolution."

"I guess. We're going away. We rented a cabin."

Cory had used his mother's card. Tonight was for gas and supplies. Toilet paper and Gatorade. He'd got the list off the internet. They'd stop at the 7-Eleven on the way. Two weeks, Cory figured. New year, new life.

"Where is it?"

"What?" She hugged herself to stop from scratching.

"The cabin."

"I don't know. I don't even want to go." There were black strings hanging from the ceiling now. She swiped at one so it wouldn't touch the baby. Footsteps above.

Miranda said, "I hate travelling this time of year too. We just drove down from Penticton."

"I'm scared of trees," she said, and Miranda laughed again.

She'll put down the baby and leave sooner if you leave. Said the angel.

"Well. Bye." She backed toward the door.

"Bye," Miranda said. "Thanks!"

When she slipped into the hallway, the urge to woof came on strong. She'd seen the can earlier and now she pushed past somebody coming out, jabbed the lock. The sink was another aggravation until she got that it was magic. You had to wave your hand to turn it on. She bowed and retched. When she looked up, mascara was melting beneath her eyes. Pupils huge, leaking blackness. With her hair down she couldn't find her real self in this stranger, which made her think of the twins cross-legged on their piece of cardboard. Nobody could tell them apart so they called them Twin One and Two. Then there was only One. Or maybe Two.

And if she did go to this cabin, which was probably just some crap motel? She leaned closer to the mirror. It was already starting to leak out through her eyes—what waited for her on the other side.

SOMEBODY TOUCHED HER arm. Fat Legs from the elevator, blowing wine breath in her face and nearly sending her right back into the can.

"Jumpy!" she said, and laughed. "Michelle. I forget your name too. All I remember is Fluevog."

Michelle saw her confusion. She pointed to the green shoes just as a tall woman in dress pants and a shiny sleeveless blouse came up and kissed her cheek. "Miranda!" Michelle squealed.

Miranda looked different standing up.

"When did you get here?" Michelle asked her.

"Like, an hour ago."

"Now I remember. Angel! This is Angel."

Miranda turned to her and smiled. "We met. She saved me."

Michelle said, "Where's that baby?"

"Sleeping. I have to find Greg. Help me. Bye, Angel. Thanks again!"

They walked off, two chicks with jiggling butts. The only thing they had to cry about.

She stopped first in the hall to switch shoes, poking a foot around in the pile until she found an approximate 7. An actual one; it was written inside in gold. Black leather flats, black leather bows. Somebody blew a noisemaker in the other room. Bye-bye green shoes. She stuffed them in the closet.

At the bedroom door, she paused. Waves of sweat. Castanet teeth. That weird plucked-at feeling. They were coming right back with Greg. She went in, grabbed the first coat in the pile that seemed her size, a puffy silver parka, cold on her arms as they entered the sleeves. The coat Cory loved was just under it. He said he loved her but if that was true, where was he?

With the elastic from her wrist she tied her hair in a top-knot. Stuck her head back out into the hall to make sure the coast was clear.

Because of the shaking, it took longer to strip the wallets and stuff her pockets. She worried too about the baby being there. Worried about him waking in a strange room.

"What do you think you're doing?"

She looked up. A man—Greg?—stood in the open door wearing glittery 2020 glasses, a basket filled with party favours hanging on one arm. One of the credit cards fell out of her pocket. She nearly heaved.

He stepped inside and, using two fingers like scissors, picked up the card and handed it to her. "Jin Hua, Official Party Animal." He lifted the glasses off. "I forbid you to leave. It's ten minutes to midnight."

It seemed then that dark hands started stirring in patterns above her. She was their marionette. She couldn't think how to get past this man and away—from the party and Cory, everything. Her hand, worked by the strings, tucked the credit card back into the pocket of the silver parka and closed the zipper. Yet some tiny part of her brain was still free, the part that knew a baby was sleeping on the other side of the room. The strings tugged her toward the door, but was the baby okay? She would worry about him all night if she didn't check, maybe for the rest of her life, which might be the same thing.

She brought her finger to her lips. The strings tightened. They wanted her to leave. Jin Hua didn't understand so she gestured. *Follow me.* Silently, they crept to the other side of the bed. Together they looked down in the crib.

Jin Hua gasped. "Oh my God!"

The baby was on his back, eyes closed, arms splayed out, hands in tiny fists. Was he breathing? She couldn't tell. The strings were pulling hard now, trying to drag her away. She jerked her arms to break them. Then—*duh*. She had scissors! Snip, snip, snip went her fingers, the way Jin Hua had shown her.

She reached down in the crib with the flat of her hand. Warmth poured off the baby. He exhaled, or Jin Hua sighed, or she did.

"So sweet," Jin Hua said. "Whose baby is it?"

The *relief*. Strangely, it wasn't like the needle. More like the beautiful feeling pouring down on her from the paramedic's blue eyes. "Taryn? Taryn? Can you hear me? Hello, Taryn! Welcome back!" He always seemed higher than her and now she knew that he was. The dim room filled with lightness and brightness, with the tinkling of bells and her own pure wish.

And Jin Hua whispered, "I think your phone's ringing."

THE PROCEDURE

KETMAN WAS DRIVING back from the clinic, wiper blades whupping across the glass, the lashings of water reminding him of a car wash and how he used to take his son, Kenny, to wash the truck. The boy would scream and giggle as the brushes whirred to life, his small hands clinging to Ketman so he wouldn't be swept away in the deluge.

So there *were* good memories of Kenny!

Just then a cyclist materialized out of nowhere, dressed all in black, begging to be hit so that he or his grieving relatives could sue. Normally Ketman would have laid into the horn, but the doctor came to mind, smiling like he was trying not to. In the clinic, his lips had compressed in his boyish face and his eyes, unlocking from Ketman's, had flicked to the side. This doc—the luck of the draw at a walk-in—was half Ketman's age and weight. Half the man that Ketman was, in other words, and that much farther from death, sitting there on his swivel stool trying half-assedly to conceal his smug amusement.

That was the moment when Ketman should have brought up what had happened to his mother, which really was suable, though Ketman had taken the high road.

"Two years ago. She went in for a knee job. Came out dead," he told the tyke doctor who was not, in fact, in the cab of the truck with him. "So I have a good reason to feel it's not worth the risk."

Ketman nodded several times, the last to his own reflection in the rear-view mirror.

SHELBY WASN'T THERE when he got home, but the cats greeted his arrival like faithful dogs whose crap you didn't have to pick up. They wove themselves around his legs— loam-coloured Linus, Muffy the calico—while Ketman checked the fridge for inspiration. He rustled around in the produce drawers, sniffed inside containers.

A few years back, to help burn off the slack season's unexpended energy, Ketman had stepped in as cook. (It was the counsellor's suggestion, so not a complete waste of money.) With Shelby's Hilroy of stained recipes as his guide, Ketman faithfully reproduced her uninteresting meals. So encouraged was he by his success, he bought a cookbook, one with a golf-shirted guy on the cover. "Guy" as in the type who held his knife and fork in fists on either side of his grub-filled plate, guarding it. Blue-eyed, muscular, stiff brush of blond hair— much like Ketman in his youth, right down to the nose destined to overwhelm his face. Ketman boiled and basted his way from Beer Dip to Bananas Foster, then struck off on his own.

At last he settled on half a butternut squash perspiring face down on a plate. Where was Shelby? The gym, probably. It would irritate her if he phoned.

The doctor had called him *Mister* Ketman. Nobody did that, not even his landscaping crew. Nobody called him Ken either. He was just Ketman, checking the cupboard now for Arborio rice. At fifty-five he must have seemed prehistoric to that smirking medical minor. Sure, the risks of the procedure were "minimal," but *puncture* was one of them.

There was nothing to do now but wait for Shelby, so Ketman went downstairs in search of televised distractions. He was still there watching the Food Network with the cats when the back door slammed an hour later.

"Shel?" he called.

"Just a sec! I'm texting Kenny!"

Ketman waited through the next commercial before transferring Muffy from lap to couch. Linus had a diagnosis, Petting Aggression, and couldn't be handled. Ketman stood, forcing the cat to leap.

Upstairs, he found Shelby in the kitchen, bags at her feet, her rain-sprinkled glasses seemingly suctioned to her forehead as she twiddled. Ketman's bratwurst thumbs were barely opposable. He'd never got the hang of texting.

"What's the matter now?"

"Exams. He's nervous." She had yet to take off her wet coat or make eye contact. Did she even remember he'd gone for a physical?

The onion waited on the cutting board. Ketman got started peeling it, wondering, not for the first time, what was the point of going away to university if you ended up texting your mother ten times a day. Yet Shelby looked so much happier when she was communicating with Kenny. In a week he'd be back for Christmas, a reunion Ketman dreaded. The kid would barely look at him. He spoke, to Ketman at least, in grunts. In fact, Ketman got more conversation out of the guys on his crew, some of whom barely knew English.

The phone blooped. Shelby lowered her glasses and gathered up her bags. "I'm just going to change," she said, walking out.

She was gone as long as it took to make the risotto and when she finally appeared, she was texting again. "Tell him we're eating," Ketman said.

"I just did."

She took her seat across from him and smiled. Though her face was thinner from all the hours she clocked now at the gym, her hair was comfortingly the same, adding inches to her height, dyed auburn to cover the grey. Ketman's moustache, chest, and stubble were still only lightly sprinkled with age. He'd gone beige instead of grey, his work-weathered skin too. He pictured his own reflection in the rear-view mirror driving home—aghast and mushroom-hued—and cut to the chase.

"I finally got that insurance thing done."

Shelby was eying her risotto. "This looks great, Ketman. But why's it orange?"

"That's the squash from last night."

Nodding, she took a bite. A root ball of hurt formed in his chest, but where in the past Ketman wouldn't even have recognized its presence, now he grabbed his mental shovel and attacked it.

"The physical. Remember?"

She glanced at her phone. "Oh, right. Everything okay?"

The doctor had provided a pamphlet. It would have been easier just to hand it to her now, but he'd left it in the truck.

Linus sashayed over. Ketman heard his motorized purring, felt soothed when Linus rubbed against his leg. He found his words. The procedure, its risks. He spared her the unspeakable *puncture*.

"What do you think?" he asked.

Shelby was forking at the risotto like she was aerating a compost heap. "What do you mean?"

"Should I have it?"

"Everybody's supposed to, right?"

"So you think I should?"

"Of course."

Ketman recalled the doctor's face. Now this matter-of-fact response from Shelby, who seemed to have forgotten what had happened to his mother. That had been a minor procedure too. The day he was supposed to pick her up, she'd phoned Ketman to say she'd been discharged early and would meet him in the waiting area. Barely an hour later Ketman walked unawares into a scrum of white coats and flowered scrubs.

"I'd have to have a general," he told Shelby.

Her dark high school eyes, magnified by the stronger prescription of her glasses, met his. Finally, some sympathy! The dregs left over from Kenny, no doubt.

"It'd take longer to recover from the anaesthesia than the procedure, Ketman. Are you worried it's going to hurt?"

"I just don't want to be awake for it," he said. "I mean, would you?"

"For heaven's sake. Do you know how many medical indignities women are subject to?"

Ping! Beside her plate, the phone lit up. Shelby pounced on it.

*

THE NEXT DAY, Ketman called the clinic. "Knock me out. That's all I ask."

The receptionist laughed and gave him a date four months away.

Christmas came and brought Kenny with it. After a couple of days of watching his adult son stretched out on the couch, laptop on his chest, body a sleeping platform for cats, Ketman asked Shelby, "The kid still can't find two socks that match?"

"So?" Shelby replied, which brought back those 150-bucks-a-pop sessions where she'd perfected this devastating syllable.

Ketman got on the computer himself and booked a last-minute, all-inclusive in Puerto Vallarta before he blew his top.

In Mexico, while Shelby and Kenny scuba dived or caught the shuttle bus to town, Ketman conversed brokenly with the groundsmen. He checked Kenny's browser history just for the hell of it and discovered yet another aspect to their generational divide: hairy pussy on one side, shaved on the other.

Halfway through the trip he observed to Shelby that she wasn't only swimming in the hotel pool, but in her bathing suit.

"I'm okay, Ketman," she said.

"Come. I want to treat you."

In the shop in the lobby, he stationed himself outside the change room. A pink one-piece. He couldn't convince her of the bikini.

"Hot mama!" Ketman told her when she emerged. Before she could escape, glaring, back into the cubicle, he stepped in front of the mirror with her.

"Look at us, Shelby. Thirty-two years and going strong." An

arm around her shoulder, he pulled her to him with the whole raw force of his love.

In the mirror Shelby's head snapped to the side, setting her glasses askew on her face.

THE DAYS GREW longer, the rain less torrential. *Galanthus, Muscari, Crocus.* Whether Shelby had finally accepted Kenny-lessness, Ketman couldn't say. He was back on the job and outside, not "breathing down her neck all day." And Shelby was too busy managing the work schedule to go to the gym. She joined a women's book club instead.

This time of year, yard maintenance overtook the design side of Ketman's business. He hired extra crew, stepped in for the no-shows. Then, after a long day power raking and pruning, he would putz in their own yard, meaning they ate dinner later. Over one of those twilight meals, Shelby brought up the procedure.

Ketman jolted in his chair. "Did they call?"

"It says on the schedule that you're supposed to confirm it," Shelby said.

Now he remembered. He'd written it down himself then apparently frittered away the months of his reprieve. He could hear that outside, among the bud-swollen *Camellia japonica*, the birds were laughing at him.

"Could you confirm it, Shel?"

She was in charge of the phone. He'd put her on the payroll around the same time she'd stopped cooking, which had made no sense to Ketman—his money was already hers—but the counsellor said to.

"No, Ketman," she said now. "It's not a work thing."

He felt his whole being sag. Elbows on the table, head propped up on his fingertips, he scrubbed worriedly at his eyebrows.

"I understand," he said, though he didn't.

The next morning, Ketman went to the room they called her office. It was decorated with Kenny memorabilia, shelves lined with dusty consolation trophies and Mother's Day crafts: tissue-paper roses in a papier-mâché vase, a pottery turd. The schedule, kept in a large rectangular hardbound book, lay open on her cluttered desk. Ketman cleared it off, replaced the cordless phone in its stand to charge, set aside the nail file and clippers. The miniature scimitars of his wife's trimmed nails he swept lovingly into his palm and deposited in the wastebasket.

Now the week spread before him, his own back-slanted hand surrounded by Shelby's sweetly looped letters. Each day was overcast with pencilled addresses and phone numbers, except for the clean coming weekend. There was nothing on the Friday, even.

Good Friday, Ketman read. *Easter Monday*.

Easter? They'd just had Christmas!

Ketman clutched the edge of the desk. He pictured the bubble gum Crocs again and his mother's legs immodestly splayed on the floor. Ketman had bought her the Crocs himself but failed to recognize them at first.

He lifted the phone back out of its stand and dialed. To the receptionist who answered, he gave his full, consonanted name, heard her clicking it on the keyboard. The funeral home had blown his mother's floral arrangements, Ketman recalled with bitterness now. He'd specified no lilies. There he'd sat in the pew, wreathed in cloying scent, stewing instead of grieving while, beside him, his brother, Mark, freely sobbed. Ketman had asked Mark to pick up their mother because he, Ketman, was supposed to be out in Langley xeriscaping an industrial park that day. Mark, whose office was twenty minutes away from the hospital, had said no. Yet if Mark *had* picked her up? She might have died in the arms of a son, her own flesh and blood, instead of surrounded by strangers.

According to the receptionist, the complicated pre-procedure instructions had been emailed to him months before. She re-sent them now, along with the list of dietary restrictions.

"Easter dinner," she said, as if the statement were a question.

"Pardon?"

"Watch the rolls. No seeds."

"Got it," Ketman said, and hung up.

KETMAN LEFT FOR work, but for the rest of the day he fretted. About the procedure. About his mother and the way she'd died. Fretting led to haranguing. One guy on his crew got surly and muttered a Punjabi expletive that Ketman knew. *Chitterchort.* Ketman blew his top.

His brother too was on his mind. Mark who only had him, Ketman, his big bro. Yet Ketman and Mark hadn't spoken in more than a year.

When he went to bed that night, he found Shelby reading her outdated feminist tome. She left the radio on all day, tuned to the CBC, and Ketman was pretty sure he'd heard that there were three sexes now, possibly more.

He asked her about inviting Mark and Sunita for Easter dinner. Shelby's eyes widened. "Seriously?"

"Remember what you said to me after mom's funeral?" Ketman asked.

Shelby didn't.

"'Mark is your flesh and blood.'" His only remaining blood relative, apart from Kenny. "Without Mom and Kenny here, what would be the point of cooking a ham? But I won't ask them if you don't want me to. We just won't do Easter."

Weariness settled in her voice and on her face. "They don't bother *me*, Ketman. And you're the one cooking."

"It will be three days before the procedure," Ketman reminded her as he got up to pee.

When he flicked on the bathroom light, the cats appeared as if by magic. Linus batted at the toilet paper hanging off the roll while Ketman stared down into the bowl. Urine streamed as from a hose. At least he had no prostate worries.

He preferred it when Shelby participated in the decision-making. Apparently, though, he overconsulted, or so she'd complained in counselling. Shelby didn't want to consult on everything. The problem was that, on his own, even when Ketman heard the *ding-ding-ding* of alarm bells that signalled an error of judgment, he ignored them.

Because, despite the *ding-ding-ding* clearly audible now over the flushing toilet, despite the fiasco of their last holiday meal with Mark and Sunita, he couldn't ignore this fact: with his procedure only six days away, it might be Ketman's Last Supper.

HAM, SCALLOPED POTATOES, minted pea soup, lemon pie. Ketman went a little crazy with the meringue. Mount Fuji in his oven. The reasonable foreboding in the concrete six-pack of his gut he'd channelled into a pussy willow centrepiece with matching sprigs for the napkin holders.

Shelby was mad at him. After hours of the silent treatment, with their guests about to arrive, she suddenly had at him again while she tucked in the pussy willow sprigs, her sole contribution to the meal as his helpmate.

"What you are, Ketman, is a bully."

His latest no-show was to blame, the worker who'd got surly a few days before. He'd called the office line that morning demanding a cheque and giving Shelby his version of what had happened, which apparently counted for more than Ketman's.

"The guy swore at me," Ketman said—again. "What do you expect me to do?"

"What did you call *him*?"

"He was dragging his ass around. How come I never get credit for *not* blowing my top? I only get demerits when I do."

The doorbell interrupted them. "Don't mention the procedure," he told Shelby. "I don't want Mark to worry."

Shelby, making a sound through her nose, went to answer the door.

There were cries of surprise from down the hall, followed by exclamations. "You've lost so much weight," Sunita said. "Isn't that he-man feeding you anymore?"

When Ketman joined them at the door, Sunita thrust the chilly bottle she was carrying into his hands. A lawyer like Mark, she was dressed in a teal-blue shalwar kameez embroidered in gilt instead of her usual drab pantsuit.

Sunita scooped up Muffy and the sisters-in-law headed for the kitchen, as though Shelby had something to do with what was happening there.

Mark had removed his shoes and now stood blandly in his socks. His grip when Ketman shook his hand was slippery and soft, as though he'd applied lotion in the car. Behind the chunky glasses, a curious look. He was probably wondering about this sudden invitation.

"Beer?" Ketman said, waving him through to the living room.

He took Sunita's prosecco to the kitchen. The moment he entered, the women fell silent. Shelby frowned. Then Sunita exclaimed, "Ketman, this pie!" She pointed to where it towered in his mother's Pyrex pan.

He took down a pair of flutes from the cupboard. Shelby and Sunita watched while he popped the cork and poured them each a glass, Sunita smiling as though she couldn't believe Ketman possessed the fine motor skills required for the task.

With two beers in hand, he left them to it.

Mark had installed himself on the living room couch, dress shirt straining across his paunch. He looked heavier, or maybe it was the beard. With a smile that seemed worked with strings, he accepted the bottle from Ketman.

"Did you want a glass?" Ketman asked.

"It's fine."

Ketman sat in an armchair, took a sip, and rested the cold bottle on his knee. Mark stared at the rug. In one room, the women were gabbing ruthlessly, in the other the men were at a complete loss. Why the hell had Ketman invited them?

Linus leapt onto his lap. Distracted by the tension, Ketman petted him. Predictably, Linus bit, prompting Ketman to react exactly the way the vet had told him not to in the case of Petting Aggression. He swore and shoved Linus off his lap. Mark puckered with disapproval.

"I'm having a procedure on Wednesday," Ketman blurted.

Mark's brows lifted above his designer frames. "What kind of procedure?"

Shelby and Sunita entered then, prosecco off-gassing in their flutes. "Is this men's talk?" Sunita asked. "Should we leave?"

Shelby dropped into the other armchair. Ketman tried to signal to her his distress, but she countered his look with one approaching dislike. He'd seen it so often since Kenny went away that it was becoming her default expression. *This* was why he'd invited Mark and Sunita. He didn't want to have Easter dinner alone with his wife.

Sunita settled next to Mark, tucking her legs under her broad rump and resting her beautiful bangled arm on his shoulder. "Oh, *the* procedure. I thought you would've had it by now, Ketman."

"Nope," he said.

"I haven't either," Shelby told Sunita. "Have you?"

"I'm only forty-eight. Mark, you should have it."

"Ketman's freaking out," Shelby said.

"I am not!" Ketman said.

But Mark nodded. "Because of Mom." He grew pensive, the sandy brows sinking below the fancy frames. Ketman could hardly believe that his brother understood him. Just as he became convinced of it, Mark put on a faux-British squawk.

"No one expects the Pulmonary Embolism!"

Everyone laughed except Ketman, who went to the kitchen to check the potatoes.

Done. Gruyère convulsed under the foil. The others were still laughing in the living room over his mother's corpse. The sooner they ate, the sooner they'd leave.

Shelby slipped into the kitchen then and pulled her phone from her cardigan pocket. "I'm wondering if he opened my Easter package yet." *Bloop* went her departing message.

Either their guests, or the prosecco, had taken the edge of her mood. She actually offered to carry in the soup. He ladled at the stove while Shelby delivered the bowls to the table, one at a time.

"It's going okay so far," she whispered on the last trip.

Ketman took his place at the head of the table, Jesus's place, and fixed his eyes on the pussy willow centrepiece.

"But seriously, Ketman," Mark said. "The procedure? Is this a fear-of-death thing?"

Partly, yes, he wanted to say. But over the last few days Ketman had begun to sense a murkier terror. He shrugged, sending Shelby a yearning glance at the same time. "I've lived a good life."

Sunita said, "Well if it's not a fear of death, then it could only be one thing."

Mark nodded. "Squeamishness."

Sunita said, "It's a challenge to his heteronormativity."

"His what?" Shelby said.

Sunita took Ketman for a redneck, which technically he was. The Redneck Gourmet. (The time she'd called him that, Ketman imagined his own cookbook with that title or, better yet, a Food Network show.) While Sunita and Mark took turns explaining Ketman's toxically masculine world view to his wife, Ketman bowed over his bowl and began delivering soup to his mouth in a steady, crank-turning motion. Impossible not to recall the fiasco of their last get-together the Christmas after their mother died. It had started jokily too, with Mark telling Kenny he was lucky to be an only child, but had ended up as a free-for-all of accusations going back to boy-hood. Sunita even brought up how Mark used to walk himself to school. "Can you imagine?" she'd told Shelby. "Six years old. A busy road to cross. Ketman was supposed to walk with him."

"There was an underpass," Ketman had said.

Yes, the underpass! The underpass with scary graffiti! No molester had been lurking there to snatch Mark. He wasn't struck by a car.

"He was lucky," Sunita said.

What next, Ketman had wondered. Mark's long-standing grievance regarding the unequal division of Halloween candy? What were these whingings compared to letting your mother die alone on a cold floor? he'd asked Mark, who, taking umbrage, made a swift and vocal exit with Sunita.

Shelby was listening to them now as she sipped her soup, wearing the same expression she wore while reading—a Rip Van Winkle fascination with everything she'd seemingly slept through. Main course, salad, then pie. And if they tried to linger, Ketman had the excuse of needing to rest up for the procedure.

He went to get the ham, wobbly as a buttock, smeared with mustard, doused in maple syrup. When he returned, Shelby finally spoke.

"Actually, you're both overthinking Ketman. He's a big baby, that's all."

Ketman released the platter two inches above the table. It thunked.

They all held out their plates for him to load.

THE NEXT DAY, Easter Monday, Ketman drove out to Delta to pick up some compost for the backyard. Shelby, in a hurry to finish her book, made it clear she didn't want him hanging around the house.

On the drive, he pondered Shelby's comment to Sunita and Mark. Had she been defending him? Possibly. But then he remembered what she'd called him when they'd argued over the no-show.

Bully.

Ketman wasn't as heteronormative as they thought, though. Not with his preference for cats over dogs. (Practically *effeminate*.) Or his cooking. He'd doted on his mother. And what about the pussy willow centerpiece he'd spent two hours creating, that not one of them had commented on?

Ketman was nearing the Massey Tunnel by then and when he realized it, he pictured himself pitted against Sunita in court, citing this further, irrefutable proof of his tender nature: every time he drove through the tunnel, he thought of Princess Di.

Irrelevant, said Sunita, who was not, in fact, in the truck with him.

No bottleneck on a holiday. Ketman breezed right through, remarking—also as usual—its untagged state, where every other stretch of bare concrete in the Lower Mainland bore the spray can's jagged testaments.

He spent an hour shovelling in the compost. Its sour aroma infiltrated the cab of the truck all the way back home.

THAT NIGHT, SHELBY claimed she wasn't hungry. So Ketman's actual Last Supper before the dreaded liquid fast was a plate of leftovers he chomped through at the counter. He swallowed the pills from the kit he'd picked up at the pharmacy, then went downstairs to pace the den.

Nothing happened.

Shelby still had a hundred or so pages to go in *The Second Sex*, eyes glued to it as he climbed into bed.

"Fasting tomorrow. You'll have to go it alone."

"I'll survive," she told him.

What happened to us, Ketman wanted to ask her then, but didn't dare.

The next morning, he concocted the slippery solution from the foil packets and drank it down. Something happened then—a purging the likes of which Ketman had never experienced. The litres sluiced through him, a car wash in the penultimate stage before the hot air starts up. But instead of being inside *it*, *it* was inside *him*. By the end of the day, he felt like a discarded rubber glove.

An image came to him, ignominiously, while he was still sitting on the throne. He pictured the Massey Tunnel again, but not clean like it actually was. The murky thing he dreaded waited there. And in the middle of those gangland ciphers, actual legible words. His full legal name and, beside it—*asshole*.

The possible jagged truth of himself, sprayed huge.

THE NEXT MORNING, Shelby dropped him off at the hospital entrance and drove away without a backward glance. Ketman rooted himself on the spot, confusing the automatic door behind him. It opened and closed, opened and closed, while he stared at the Honda's blinking indicator. He couldn't see Shelby. She was shorter than the headrest. The car merged into the flow of traffic, then vanished.

Signs pointed the way to *Gastro-enter-ology*, where they handed him a gown. In the change room, his thick fingers struggled with the ties, then the weird socks and their no-slip fish scales. Clothes, wallet, and phone loaded into the plastic drawstring bag.

A large, regal, grey-permed nurse handed him a clip-boarded form to fill out in the intake area across from the nursing station. A few minutes later she came over and saw his shaking hands.

"You must be cold."

She returned with a blanket, which she tenderly spread across his lap. With the majesty of a cruise ship berthing, she slid her bulk into the chair beside him, took back the clip-board, cooed the questions, and ticked the boxes on his behalf. Checked his pulse and wrote it down. Ketman thought of his mother's loving ministrations, the honey-sweetened aspirins crushed in a spoon, the thermometer slipped under his tongue.

"Please," he said. "I have to talk to my wife."

The phone was at the very the bottom of the drawstring bag. The nurse found it for him.

"What?" Shelby answered.

Ketman heard café sounds in the background. She'd said something about meeting someone for lunch. "Come back, Shel."

"I'll be there at three like I'm supposed to be."

"Now. *Please*."

"Ketman? It's a colonoscopy. Grow up."

She hung up before he could speak of his love, before he could vow to submit again to the counsellor and her pitiless judgments, submit to anything Shelby wanted. He loved Kenny too, he wanted to say. Of course he did! It was just that Kenny irritated Ketman, much the way he, Ketman, irritated Shelby.

"Better now?" the nurse asked.

She escorted him to the holding area beyond the nursing station. A half-dozen beds separated by curtains. He lay down. Another nurse took charge of him there, cheery and round-faced, who lifted his hand and began gently slapping the back of it, as though to scold him. She was coaxing out his veins. The IV port slid right in.

"You're putting me under, right?" Ketman said.

"You'll get a sedative. You might fall asleep."

"I asked to be knocked out," he told her.

Another gurney wheeled in, bumping Ketman into the hall. As they traded places, Ketman saw the back of the incoming patient curled on his side. Deflated shoulders, the freckled top of his bald head with a wispy brown fringe beneath it. He seemed shrunken. Destroyed.

They left Ketman, whose breathing came now in fishlike gasps. Crepe-soled orderlies brisked back and forth. A poster hung on the wall above him. He read it to calm himself. Code Grey: Disruptive Individual. Code Green: Internal Evacuation. *Ding-ding-ding-ding-ding.*

Then a new face loomed above him, young and rosy, his actual nurse. Staring up at her nose-ringed innocence, Ketman understood that his mortification would be boundless. "I want a general," he whimpered.

A gapped smile. "You'll be fine," she said.

The nurse wheeled him across the hall into a huge, night-black room where the blinking eyes of the machines in one corner were the only source of light.

"Turn onto your left side, please, Mr Ketman."

The doctor must have come in then, or she'd been lurking in the shadows the whole time. She introduced herself, placing a warm hand on his shoulder.

"How do you feel, Mr Ketman?"

"I asked for a general. They said it would be okay."

"Why? Don't you want to watch?"

She began rattling off the terms of consent. Hearing that word again—*puncture*—Ketman gave up. Meanwhile, the nurse was fiddling with the IV. He felt the vein in his hand stretching to accommodate an incoming flow, distracting him from the same intrusion elsewhere, the actual *chitterchort*.

A scene bloomed on the monitor just above his head. He knew the place. He'd been there, either in a nightmare or in one of those computer games he used to play with Kenny. A long pulsing passage glistening with moisture.

"All right, Mr Ketman. Here we go."

There are mysteries. Drowsy already, less agitated, Ketman accepted their existence though his inclination had always been not to dig too deep, to stay in the topsoil, far from life's profundities. He wasn't interested, preferred instead the beige surface of things because, in the end—was that what this was, the end?—his life, however unexamined, satisfied him. Shelby, the cats. Business was good. Kenny might come round. Ketman didn't have huge expectations. His one complaint? He missed his mother.

"Here's the first corner."

He saw it up ahead, a bend, and now a sour taste flooded his mouth and he wanted to call out to the doctor to slow down, but his tongue only lolled, he, too, helplessly under the control of she-who-moved-the-cursor. She was pushing him deeper inside his own slimed coils, into the more distant loops where his fear had organized itself into that monstrous shape, where it squatted in the extended cave of who he actually was. Except, when he did round the corner, the same pink walls came into view.

"You're doing great."

Maybe it was relief, but he sensed a different presence now, not malignant, the opposite, an almost universal benignity, a protecting and fostering spirit maternally gathering him up, his own mother in fact, here with him, always, even in his colon, infusing him to the cellular level with such a ludicrous sense of hope that when the next corner appeared he abandoned all resistance and moved glad-heartedly toward it, so certain was he that she would be there when he rounded that curve—smiling, her heavy arms open, glasses fogged from the humidity. She understood and loved him. She loved him best.

She wasn't there. His disappointment gave way to shock, then to the shocking truth of her absence. Its permanence. He dug in his feet to stop himself, but got no purchase from the socks. What had he been thinking? His mother would never come *here*, not with her lifelong distrust of germy places, especially public toilets—which was secondary to the fact that she was dead.

Dead, dead, dead, dead, dead, dead, dead.

"We're near the end, Mr Ketman. It'll be over in a moment."

He wanted to close his eyes, but couldn't. Around, then around again to the penultimate bend until he saw it hunkering ahead—the thing he dreaded. Ketman was alone with it. Ketman alone.

HOMING

Part Two

IN THE RENTAL listing the house looked as rudimentary as a child's drawing: a square with a door in the middle, a window on either side. For a roof, a triangle. Marta pictured her son, Peter, at a long-ago kitchen table rendering it in blue wax crayon. (Peter was an investment banker now in Basel with his own child, a baby, whom Marta had only seen on WhatsApp, never held.)

"There's even a shed out back," the agent told her on the phone.

Marta detected sarcasm. He'd spent most of the conversation extolling other listings, like the bloated faux-Tudor in the subdivision, similar to what she lived in now. Newish, with five bedrooms, it commanded significantly more rent than this Crayola playhouse. But apart from a bit of furniture, which the college was paying to move, she was only bringing what would fit in her car.

While still on the phone, she took a Google Street View

walk around the Crayola house's neighbourhood. Other old-timers (bigger, with porches and vinyl siding) mingled with 70s split-levels. At the end of the block, she came to a drab, stuccoed building, a Wellness Centre according to the sign, offering mental health and addiction services. Its proximity didn't particularly trouble her, especially when her cursor led her to a river unfurling itself just two streets away.

Marta was sixty-two and she carried the accumulated weight of these years stylishly, in drapey clothes and big, amber-framed progressives. Even during mask mandates, she kept up her bright lipstick. This move was temporary, an intentional disruption after the non-event of her separation from Glen. The non-affair of it, she'd told Peter on WhatsApp— because there wasn't one to make the breakup comprehensible to him, or interesting.

Peter said he got it. "You and Dad ran out of things to say a decade ago. Then you had to spend eighteen months together under house arrest."

The last part was an understandable exaggeration; lockdown had been harsher in Europe. The rest was pretty accurate.

"I'll take the Crayola house," she told the agent.

"Which?"

FOR ONE YEAR she would be the interim director of human resources at a community college in Caribou Arm, a resource town up north. Everyone said she was crazy, that the job wasn't a step down from her current position but a three-flight tumble. She should use her leave to travel, go to Europe and see her grandson. Or have the affair that she'd missed out on, the one that had not precipitated her separation.

"Travel?" Marta had sputtered. And find herself intubated in Lisbon, or Zagreb? She didn't want to intrude on Peter and Marcel in these precious early months either, or butt against the Swiss *grandmère*. As for an affair, sex was about as satisfying now as the trek to the community mailbox: all that puffing and sweating, only to find a crumpled Domino's flyer in her box. And look who was advising her! Friends she hadn't seen since the start of the pandemic, who, without a restaurant table to convene at, couldn't be bothered to keep in touch.

Glen would stay in the house during her absence; when she returned, they'd decide whether or not to sell. Though technically no longer a couple, they were still in each other's bubble, so the morning of her departure, they hugged. In the middle of it, an impulse seized Marta: to noogie him like she used to when they were dating. Back then he'd had more hair. Her rings scratched and he pulled back with a yelp.

"What the hell, Marta?"

She drove off, Glen still in the driveway, not waving, but checking his bald spot for blood. He was an accounting instructor; feelings baffled him, or Marta's did.

What Marta felt now was an elation that lasted the full nine hours of the drive. Mountains flattened, forests conceded to grassland. Sixteen-wheelers rode her tail. Let them!

But then she arrived and took her first wobbly step inside the Crayola house. Other renters had obviously come and gone since the online pictures had been taken, scuffing and dinting both ways. They'd left their traces in lidless Tupperware, a toilet brush, a fraying doormat, the proverbial Domino's flyers. Dismal artifacts of a waning civilization. Inside the door of the smaller bedroom, a ballpoint ladder charted a child's growth. Marta stared at the last date, unable to believe that 2020 was an actual year, let alone one already in the past. What just happened? Her life?

The promised shed was raised up on concrete blocks, an unsightly raw wood scar on one side, as though some part of it had been ripped away. She noticed, too, that it smelled decidedly peculiar. Ammonic. The movers stashed two kitchen chairs there.

Last to be unloaded was her loveseat. In the dollhouse living room, Marta sat with ringed hands folded in her lap. A dog barked in some nearby yard, over and over.

"What have I done?" she asked.

Already conversing with herself!

THE COLLEGE WAS across the river on the edge of a nondescript cinder-block downtown. By contrast, it was bright and new, designed after a traditional Dakelh pit house with a trapezoidal facade of glass and logs. The dress code was casual, more casual than Marta's interactions with her staff who, in all fairness, couldn't be blamed for their reserve. Some of them had probably applied for her job. The fact that everyone was younger and masked didn't help.

Every day after work she unwound with the walk she'd first taken on Google, leaving now by the front door. Directly across was a rancher with a junk-jammed carport, where a couple in their forties (white where they weren't tattooed) lived with a vocal dog named Gorilla, the one she'd heard the first day and every day since. Marta hadn't spoken to them, just heard them yelling at the dog, who was penned or chained out of view. The black monster parked in the driveway probably got more attention than Gorilla, and more washing.

As she walked, she swung her arms. It burned more calories and gave her a freer feeling, a determined feeling, as though she had a purpose. Instead of fences, trees or feral lilacs demarcated most of the yards. Lilacs were spring bloomers, a season that probably came late here. June? Would she see them bloom? Would she actually make it that long?

These doubtful calculations suddenly squeezed the air out of her—hard. She had to stop mid-stride, one hand over her connipting heart. She thought she was going to faint. Eventually, though, the panic subsided and she lurched on.

If she had collapsed, how long would she have lain there? Apart from the people directly across from her, neighbour sightings were rare. Whenever she did encounter someone unloading groceries from their trunk or mowing the lawn, they offered no more than a perfunctory nod. In fact, the only remotely sociable exchange happened when she passed the Wellness Centre, where the smokers in the parking lot paused their collegial disputations to wave as she strode by—if she waved first, that is. Otherwise, nothing.

It only took a few days to conclude this wasn't pandemic skittishness, but the culture of the place, like driving a pickup.

At the river, the trees on both banks shimmered in their late-summer greens. A slope of grass gave way to a spiked band of reeds, then the steely fast-flowing water. Marta sat on a bench, ignored by other people taking their constitutionals. Did they think she was crazy, or was invisibility simply the lot of unpartnered women of a certain age? Not that she cared for the time being. She'd come here to face her solitude. *That* was her purpose after twenty-eight years of marriage. Not to run from it, but to meet it head-on. However, if part 2 of her life was always going to be like this, she already knew she'd need a part 3.

In truth, she'd been alone for a long time, possibly since her mother died ten years before, an event that Marta had experienced as the ultimate severing of the umbilical cord. Peter had already flown the coop. Only Glen had been there, tiptoeing in the background, while Marta lamented her various sins of omission.

A MONTH AFTER her arrival, she broke down and made an appointment at the SPCA, a five-minute drive from the college, which nonetheless went awry. When Marta finally showed up, she was met by a grey-haired woman in a face mask printed with a terrier's snout. Above the fanged smile, the stink eye— for lateness, or just because. Kittens were on offer, but Marta didn't think she was up to the challenge. She picked a grown cat, ebony, with a sultry slow blink.

Once home, she learned what those citrine eyes had actually been saying: *Lady, I'm going to stick my ass in your face every chance I get.* During dinner, he jumped on the table so she could admire his posterior over her single-portion meal. He did the same when she got into bed that night, kneading the pillow of her stomach as she was trying to read. She picked her phone off the nightstand and texted a picture of the cat's ass to Peter.

Look what I got!

Peter countered with Didier, her grandson, diaperless on the change table, waving his perfect legs in the air.

She remembered the advice she'd eschewed. If she'd gone to Basel, she could have been munching on those fat legs now. Why had she denied herself? Did she think she didn't deserve it? She turned out the light, bracing for another moody, tearful night.

The cat, still unnamed, dissolved in the darkness.

In the morning, when she opened the kitchen door to eat her breakfast in the sun, he dashed into the lilac wilderness, never to moon her again.

A CHASM OPENED inside Marta after that. During work hours, she could pretend, but once home, the frenzied clicking began: *Add to Cart, Add to Cart, Add to Cart*...In went the Neapolitan novels (those Italians!), kindergarten-coloured paint (a different shade for every room). A kit to knit a baby blanket, and warmer clothes in various sizes—because she didn't know if she'd get out of there thinner or fatter, if at all. iBird and binoculars for her river walks. With each purchase, she stuck her head into the void and listened.

There Was No Bottom.

Come October, she was near tears all the time, as well as angry with herself. The interim director of human resources had none!

"Imagine. My parents immigrated here—to Canada, I mean—in the 50s," she mused to a random checkout clerk. "They knew no one, owned nothing."

"Can you please stay behind the Plexiglas?" the girl replied.

Marta wheeled her overfull cart out of the store, hands shaking.

It confounded her, this void. After all, if she'd stayed in the Venn diagram of her marriage, she and Glen would have been living in their amicable circles (Marta with her cryptic crosswords and *Inspector Morse*, Glenn his hockey-watching and vinification), overlapping mainly at mealtimes. Were things so different? Apparently, because when Glen phoned now it was all Marta could do not to crumble, not to *succumble* to fond revisionism. Previous irritants topped the list of things she actually missed: his noisy breathing, the bubbling carboy in the downstairs bathroom (varietal: Urine Sample). His childish pouting every time she made that joke. How to explain the contradiction of her loneliness when she'd been the one to leave? She couldn't even describe it. To say it haunted her— it was always in her face, like the ass of a cat—wasn't right. Haunting suggested a presence. Negative space did have a shape. It was formed by the things that were there. There was so much there for Marta! She was privileged in every way! Now it had all been shoved to the periphery to make room for this unbearable...what?

Nights were the worst. She had to shut her phone in the nightstand so she wouldn't keep checking the time. Only minutes passed, never hours.

Near the end of one marathon of wakefulness, she thought she heard a sound—a sort of thrumming, like from a transmission tower, but pitched lower. It seemed to be coming from a long way off. As it grew louder, and possibly closer, layers were added. Burbling? Swishing? It became mysterious.

Marta sat up. It was definitely coming closer. Flying closer. Airplane? Drone? UFO? The dog across the street began barking. Marta fumbled in the drawer for her phone, only to drop it with a shriek when something struck the roof. The time illuminated in her lap was 6:23.

A long volley of thumps followed, which made her think, absurdly, of reindeer alighting. An animal that large would probably crash right through. Was it an animal? Why not angels? Oh, she was dreaming! *I'm asleep*, she thought with relief.

The thumping ceased. Now she heard gurgling and scratching. Should she go out? The mornings bit now and, anyway, whatever was up there soon fell silent, along with Gorilla.

She lay back down. Even if there was no sign of it when she got up, she'd still know it had been real. The dog had heard it too.

Part Three

NOCTURNAL TOSSING TURNED her nightie into a flannel tourniquet. Marta untwisted it and, slipping on shoes, went outside.

Pigeons?

A dozen or so were quadrilling on the roof, ashy chests puffed, cloisonné necks glinting. A subgroup had gathered on the shed. What was going on? She looked across the street to the unneighbourly couple's roof. They had a tarp thrown over half of it, weighed down with bricks.

It happened to be Saturday, so Marta dressed and, without bothering with her face, set off to see how many other neighbours had received a visitation. At the Wellness Centre someone was unlocking the door—a tall, light-skinned Black man in a maroon puffer jacket, a zippered portfolio tucked under his arm.

"Hi!" Marta called. "I'm sorry to bother you, but there are all these pigeons on my roof. It's...unnerving."

"I'm just opening up here," he called back.

Resigned now to these rebuffs, Marta walked on. By the end of her scouting mission, she knew she'd been singled out.

Back home, while she made coffee, she pondered the Holy Spirit, specifically how it was represented in old paintings. What was that *Annunciation* she'd seen at the Met? A Flemish

Mary flanked by angels. She'd looked perfectly serene despite the dove coming in for a landing on her head. But these birds weren't white; they were grey with iridescent touches. Ordinary Feathered Rats. Yet Marta felt giddy. Hadn't she thought of angels the previous night?

On the other hand . . . She shuddered: *The Birds*. Still, the joyful feeling remained. Now she had something interesting to tell Peter next time they WhatsApped.

Instead of her river walk, she pulled one of the chairs out of the smelly shed. This caused the breakaway group to lift off in an explosion of flapping before resettling exactly where they'd been. Positioned to watch both roofs, she consulted iBird while she drank her coffee. *Columba livia*, a.k.a. rock pigeon. They paced and bobbed in random patterns, almost mechanically, like windup birds with bright glass beads for eyes. All the while they kept up their soothing, low-pitched burble. Eventually the smaller faction on the shed fell into line, all facing the same direction, toward Marta, like theatregoers waiting for the play to start.

Someone behind her delivered the first line. "You weren't lying."

She swung around in the chair, disturbing the pigeons, who then rose with her. It was the man from the Wellness Centre, accompanied by a youth wearing a ball cap and jeans with a precarious hold on his hips.

For a moment the three of them watched the birds. Bemusement had already supplanted Marta's disbelief. On the faces of the other two—the younger heavy-browed and pimpled, the older with delicate, elongated features—she saw perplexity.

She offered coffee, telling them not to bother with the masks that they were dutifully fishing out of pockets. "We're outside."

When she returned with the mugs, the youth, introduced as Brandon, pointed out that some of the birds were banded.

"What?" Marta went for a closer look, which sent the shed faction into the air again and caused her human visitors to duck under their arms. She went back inside for her binoculars.

Yes! Tiny blue bracelets!

"Should we get to the bottom of this?" Yonas, the Wellness worker, asked. A slight singsong accent added to his teasing charm. He handed his mug to Brandon and, in a slow, foxy slink, approached the shed while the birds watched, heads tilting. When he was eye to eye with them, he extended a finger. One of the banded ones rushed over and pecked it.

"That didn't hurt at all, little buddy. How about let's get along?"

Marta glanced at the boy, Brandon, who was grinning so wide she could see his whole dental catastrophe. Yonas made a platform of his hand. The bird hopped on! Marta couldn't believe it. But as his hand began to close, it beat its wings and flew off.

"They'll probably leave in a few days," Yonas told Marta, flapping his long arms. "Migration time."

MARTA SLEPT IN the next morning thanks to the soporific percolations filtering through the ceiling. The moment she stepped out the back door, her avian guests began talking excitedly, like a crowd of autograph-seekers. They gawked at her, then milled and strutted, shaking their green and purple spangles. A bunch of pigeons, scourge of the public space. The roof looked like a spatter painting.

The Thing With Feathers!

She remembered Yonas's comment about migration. Already the leafy treasury by the river was amassing gold on both its banks. But did pigeons migrate? She pulled out her phone and saw that she'd slept through a call from Peter. Reversing the camera, she called him back.

Peter's new-father face appeared, haggard and joyful in the Swiss lamplight, baby Didier asleep on his shoulder. His view was of the Crayola roof.

"Where *are* you? Trafalgar Square?"

Marta told him the whole story—the strange sound, how she'd woken the next day as the Chosen One. "And I finally met some neighbours. Two nice fellows from the addiction centre."

"See, Mom? You've just been hanging out in the wrong places. You can do this."

Didier began to grouse. Peter hooked a finger in the back of his diaper and peered inside. "Crap, Mom. I've got to go. Catch up later?"

Though she signed off with a laugh, the *you can do this* made her cringe. He was cheering her on, like she used to during his sodden soccer years, or when he wanted to invite a boy to grad. They'd reversed positions.

Had Marta been too hovery a mother? Perhaps. The person who'd suffered the most for it, though, wasn't Peter, but her own mother. She wouldn't have said so, of course. Neither of Marta's parents had abided complaining. But why hadn't they talked about something other than Peter?

She went inside and made toast, which she ate while watching the birds through the kitchen window. She'd already noticed that they would occasionally switch places too—the ones on the house would visit the shed, and vice versa. Other than this, they showed no sign of leaving.

iBird said pigeons didn't migrate. She felt a rush of relief, irrational and undeserved.

THOUGH MARTA FEARED their entrenchment, the impulse to press food and drink on visitors turned out to be innate. (Her mother's legacy: a freezer stuffed with decades of frost-burnt baking.) On her ill-fated SPCA visit, she'd passed an agricultural store, which she successfully drove to now.

"Will this do for pigeons?" she asked, hefting a sack of chicken feed onto the counter.

Instead of a mask, the clerk wore a bandana, outlaw-style. "Do they have wings? A beak? Are they stupid? Or try a pet store."

"It's temporary," Marta told him.

Back home, the sight of her lifting the sack out of the trunk caused a tizzy. Not stupid! She slit it open, tossed the seed and corn kernels around in a self-consciously folksy way, then went in search of something to fill with water.

As soon as she set the baking pan on the ground, two birds hopped in and commenced splashing. Others crowded around, waiting their turn. While they busied themselves with their ablutions, Marta opened the shed to stash the seed. It was rapidly filling up: the two extra kitchen chairs, five cans of unopened paint, cat carrier and kitty litter, the empty boxes she was saving for her return. And she saw, as if for the first time, the inner mesh door and wire-covered window, the box-like shelving. Finally, she identified that peculiar ammonic smell.

"Out!" she told the first bird that followed her inside. It hopped up on a shelf. Others came streaming in. She had to fetch a rolled-up newspaper to evict them.

So. Not special. She hadn't been singled out. These pigeons bore no tidings, biblical or otherwise. The shed was a coop, theirs apparently.

She phoned the rental agent. "I'll arrange for an exterminator," he told her.

"No!" Marta cried. "Some have bands. I looked them up and—"

"They're banded? You've got to call Wildlife Protection."

"They're not wild." She pictured the one balancing on Yonas's palm and shook her head in wonderment again. "I think they're homing pigeons."

"Weird."

"I know! Could you ask the owner if they're his?"

It took about ten minutes for him to return the call. By then Marta had left the house for her walk, glancing over her shoulder at the birds, who were staying put.

"Not his pigeons."

"When did he buy the house? Maybe they belong to the owner before him."

He didn't want to bother his client again on the weekend and Marta herself conceded that this was a Monday problem.

After several false starts and a YouTube video, she managed to cast on Didier's blanket and knit a few rows. She fed the birds before she fed herself, checked the overnight temperature before going to bed. Three degrees Celsius. They'd be fine.

The following afternoon the rental agent called as Marta was leaving a meeting. She was, in fact, preparing to recruit her permanent successor.

"He died."

"What?" Marta said. "Who?"

"The guy who owned the house. The current owner says he bought it from the daughter."

Marta stepped into her office and closed the door. "When was this?"

"I'm not sure, but I've been handling this property for three years."

After she hung up, she sat down at her desk. She'd been thinking about her parents so often lately that mention of death and a daughter could only stir up that dormant grief. She pinched her leaky nose through the mask. Then the feeling passed. Annoyance replaced it. What was *she* supposed to do about the birds? Now she'd have to face the terrier woman from the SPCA, which was possibly more of a reason to cry.

Only later, driving across the steel truss bridge at the end of the day, did the puzzlement return. The owner of the house, who'd presumably also owned these birds, had died at least three years ago. Why had they returned now?

Marta turned onto her gap-toothed street. As she neared the Crayola house, she braked.

On the patch of gravel where she normally parked stood her unneighbourly neighbour, the distressed back of her leather jacket facing Marta. A hybrid could creep up on you like this.

Marta waited, watching the birds herself, and the woman, whom she didn't want to rile. Her name was Janice frequently shortened to Jan, Marta had easily overheard. She wore a grey toque over a straggly blond ponytail, and tractor-tire boots. Marta was only a little afraid of her.

Janice did something then—spread wide her arms and

rushed at the coop, which caused the birds to lift into the autumn sky, the ones on the roof of the house too. "Go!" she added with savage gesticulations when they made to resettle. "Get out of here!"

Marta pulled in next to Janice, who looked embarrassed to have been caught on the property. "Those are Mr Bogdanovic's pigeons," she said when Marta got out of the car. It sounded like an accusation.

Close like this, Marta saw that, though younger, Janice's rutted face hinted at a harder life, one possibly lived outside. She might have been a tree-planter at one time, or unhoused.

"I was trying to track him down to tell him. I only just heard he'd died."

"What?" Janice snapped. "Who said that?"

"The rental agent."

"That's bullshit." She stomped across the street, already yelling to her partner, whose name, Marta well knew, was Wes. "Wes! Did Mr B. die?!" The unseen Gorilla started barking.

Janice went inside, leaving the front door ajar. Marta awaited intelligence. A moment later Janice reappeared. "Wes says he's still at Sugarloaf Lodge!"

"Great!" Marta called back. "Where's that?"

AN ASSISTED LIVING facility. Due to health restrictions, Marta wasn't allowed to visit Mr Bogdanovic, but the person who answered said she'd see if he was available to come to the phone.

"They just had their supper. He might be sleeping it off."

While Marta waited—a long time—she could hear the background din of dishes being cleared and television news cranked loud. Some elder, who might have been past the point of human speech, was ululating, while someone else, a staff person maybe, made cheerfully mundane remarks in that tone reserved for the four-legged, or the very old or very young. Finally, after several painful knocks of the receiver against something hard, a groggy voice said, "Hello?"

"Hi, is that Mr Bogdanovic?" Marta asked.

He cleared his throat. "Yes. Who's calling?" Now the voice sounded deep and authoritative, almost martial, especially contrasted with the sad warbling in the background.

Marta explained that she was renting his former house, and about the sudden appearance of the birds, which she was looking at through the kitchen window.

His formality fell away with his surprise. "Get away! Claude Pettit owns my birds now. What are they doing back there?"

"It seems they escaped. Should I call this other person? Do you have a number?"

"I wish I did! I'd like to know what the hell happened."

"I guess I could look him up."

"What the hell? How many?"

By then Marta had managed to count them. "Nineteen."

"That's it?"

She could hear him breathing loudly and wondered if someone was with him. How old was he? How mobile? Meanwhile, outside the window, the birds sidled closer to each other as the sky behind them ripened.

"Would you like me to call you back when I've tracked down…"

"I want to come and see them," Mr Bogdanovic interrupted.

"All right. When would you like to visit? I finish work at five."

"ASAP," Mr Bogdanovic said, back to his commandeering tone. "Tomorrow. I'll be ready at five."

They had not been having a private conversation. The woman who'd answered the phone got on the line again to explain about the health restrictions. Only the designated visitor could escort a resident off the premises.

"And that's new," she said. "Until a few months ago they weren't allowed out at all."

"Okay. Who's Mr Bogdanovic's designated visitor?"

It was his daughter, who lived in Toronto. There was an application process should the daughter agree to transfer the designation. A form-pusher herself, Marta didn't bother explaining that it would be a one-off outing.

First evening had made silhouettes of the old man's birds. Now darkness erased them altogether. Marta crept outside and, trying not to disturb them, swapped the baking pan for a Tupperware container. She gave the pan a good scrub, then made her mother's apple cake, the recipe for which lived in her heart. Once it had cooled, using her phone as a flashlight, she carried it across the street.

Wes answered the door, looking like an inflatable biker with a leak. Moustache, tooled-leather belt. Often he sported a pirate bandana, though not tonight. Tonight his hair, thinning on top, hung down to his shoulders in colourless straggles. Where Janice had several inches on him, Marta probably had forty pounds.

"Whoa!" he said of the cake. "What's this?"

"I'm Marta from across the street. Is Janice here?"

Janice came suspiciously to the door, exchanging places with Wes, who took the cake away. Marta would probably never get her pan back.

She explained why she'd come. "Do you know his daughter? I doubt she'd sign the form for me, a complete stranger, but she might for you."

"I know her," Janice said, narrowing her eyes and crossing her bare, blue-blurred arms. Marta suspected this stance had more to do with her feelings for Ms Bogdanovic, possibly the outrage of her residing in Toronto, than for Marta herself. "I'll get her to sign for *me* because, like, you're a stranger to me too, right?"

Marta, literally the new girl on the block, felt it again—the determined shunning she seemed to receive everywhere. But wasn't dealing with prickly people in her job description? She smiled. And because she hadn't been invited inside but stood in the cold with her face mask dangling from one ear, Janice received the full benign force of it.

"My name's Marta."

Janice sniffed. "Janice." She thumbed over her shoulder. "Wes."

"Good cake!" Wes yelled.

Marta went back to her apple-scented house, satisfied. More so when, a half an hour later, there was a knock. Janice held out Marta's pan, washed and dried.

"I left her a message. I'll let you know what she says."

AS THOUGH THE cake had summoned her, Marta's mother appeared in her dream that night, bustling ahead, white cap of hair glowing. Always so busy! Marta tried to catch up, but it seemed that she, Marta, had a child by the hand. Was it Peter slowing her down? His grip felt sticky. *Where are you going?* she called, but her mother had been quite deaf at the end. And then it was too late.

A bittersweetness suffused her waking. It stayed the whole day. On the drive home Marta usually listened to the news, but today she let the feeling be her passenger. A little weepy, but without any of that pre-pigeon hysteria, she steered through the broad-streeted downtown, over the bridge, onto River Road. Passing the Wellness Centre, she caught sight of Yonas in the parking lot, braked, and lowered the passenger window.

"Mystery solved!" she called.

He turned but didn't recognize her in her car.

"It's Marta!"

"They're gone?" he called back.

"Not yet! Soon!"

A few minutes after Marta pulled up at the Crayola house, Yonas did too, in a dented grey Nissan pickup. Marta was just coming out of the house with fresh water for the birds.

Yonas leaned on the open door of his truck, looking from the roof of the house to the coop. "I wanted to say goodbye. Seeing them the other day, I felt so happy. How they're all together like that? It's been a long time, right?"

He meant, Marta knew, the social bubbles and limits on gatherings. "It sure has."

She told him about Mr Bogdanovic, who was coming on Saturday to collect his birds. "You and Brandon should drop by."

"Maybe we will," he said as he waved goodbye.

"Wait!" Marta called. There were chicken pieces marinating in the fridge. "Can I make you dinner? If you don't need to get home, that is."

With Yonas's acceptance, the awkward negotiations began. Should they eat outside? Sit apart? Marta, who'd been so cautiously rule-abiding, suddenly didn't care that he worked with kids who probably disregarded every one of them. She asked for five minutes to tidy up. The strewn evidence of her shopping habit, the lipstick-stained face masks that so resembled soiled panty liners—all tossed into the spare room, the door closed.

When she came back out, Yonas was by the coop cupping a bird to his chest, murmuring to it in an unfamiliar language. Just a flow of sounds to her, it struck her as pigeon-like. He turned to her.

"You try."

Tentatively, Marta approached. He transferred the bird to her cupped hands. Claws pricked, but the overwhelming sensation was of fragility. She held her breath, shoulders hunched as high as her ears. Was she squeamish, or afraid? Of what? After a minute, she released the bird to the air.

Inside, Marta put on the rice while Yonas sat at the table with a beer. The thing about pigeons, he told her, was that they spread themselves the world over. "I chased them as a boy in Asmara."

"That's in Eritrea, right? On the Red Sea," Marta said.

"Very good. Most people have never heard of it."

"Now and then it's in the crossword puzzle," Marta admitted, which made him laugh.

"I saw the same pigeons in the Sahara Desert, and in Israel. Then Vancouver. When I came up here? I think you haven't been here long, right? You might not know how cold it gets. How could they live in those hot places and here too?"

"Same way as you?" Marta said, and he laughed again.

She asked the questions she thought wouldn't be too prying. When did he leave? Eighteen years ago. He managed to cross the border and not get shot. After a long limbo in Israel, Canada accepted his refugee application.

"My mother was a refugee," Marta told him, surprising herself with how easily she produced this near-forgotten fact. "When she was four, she was sent to Britain with the Kinder-transport."

She had to explain what the Kindertransport was. A child so young sent to live with strangers. Thank God, for none of that side of Marta's family survived.

"I only learned about it when I was ten," she told him. "My parents took me to England, where they'd emigrated from."

Marta remembered the trip as a rainy shuttle between damp, peculiar-smelling houses, relieved by the occasional sight of a castle or a bobby. Granny Blank with the snaggle-tooth wasn't her real granny, they'd told her. All she'd felt was relief—because of the terrifying tooth. They never went back. Gone to rack and ruin, her father said of the country. Good riddance!

"I'd always thought of her as British," Marta told Yonas. "Like my dad. Because she'd grown up there, she acted like it. They told me this shocking thing and I was too young to realize what it meant. I don't think it ever came up again. I certainly never asked."

Yonas shrugged. "Children aren't interested in their parents' lives."

"But I never asked her as an adult either. I was so busy with work and raising my son, and now she's dead. It's"—she slid the pan out of the oven, set it on the stove—"unforgivable."

She managed to offer Yonas a second beer and pour herself a glass of wine. He seemed to sense she was staving off tears. Of course he did. He spent his day with emoting adolescents. How mortifying to invite him in only to force more of the same on him.

When she finally stopped bustling, he said, "Maybe my scale is different, but most things are forgivable. Your problem is that the person you want forgiveness from isn't around."

Marta nodded, then had to say, "Excuse me for a moment?"

In the bathroom, she leaned over the sink, tap running so he wouldn't hear her weeping. How near the surface this sliver had been. Barely a squeeze and it popped right out of its guilty pustule. When she finally lifted her face, the tear-washed hag in the mirror snapped her to herself. A splash of water, a peony flourish of lipstick. Glasses back on, she fluffed her hair and returned to the table more or less the way she'd left. Except not.

"Sorry about that."

Yonas absolved her with a wave.

As she served him, he muttered in his singsong accent that he could believe in God again. Didn't Marta have a husband?

"I'm separated. That's why I'm here. You?"

"I'm separated too." His soft gaze returned to his food. "My wife's in jail. She didn't get across."

For a time they ate in silence, Marta first muted by shock, then blushing with shame over her earlier outburst. Meanwhile, Yonas's long fingers worked the utensils as delicately as he'd handled the bird.

"Do you hear from her?" she finally asked.

"No. I don't know where she is. There are so many prisons." A bitter chuckle. He still didn't raise his eyes. "Her sister's in Sweden now. She spoke to someone who said he thought he saw her. So I live in hope."

"I'm sorry," Marta said.

Yonas nodded at his plate.

"You know," she said after another moment. "I've never told anyone about the Kindertransport."

"Sometimes it's easier to talk to strangers."

"I haven't found that here. I'm just sorry you're the one I ended up burdening."

"You didn't," he said, looking up now. Then he smiled. "I remember my first year here. Hard. But the people are really good. They're just slow to trust city folk. So many go down to Vancouver and come back dragging new problems with them."

When they finished eating, Yonas declined coffee, but insisted on helping with the dishes. Marta imagined the birds watching them through the window as she'd so often watched them: the stout woman who fed them, passing dripping plates to this gorgeous, willowy man. He dried each one thoroughly, then placed it in the cupboard.

Afterward, they exchanged numbers. At the door, Yonas asked, "The bird who brought the little branch to Noah? What would you call it?"

"A dove."

"Is it different than a pigeon?"

"Not really."

Yonas, in Tigrinya, meant "dove."

After he left, Marta looked up prisons in Eritrea. They used shipping containers, or underground caves. Everyone shackled together in darkness. Too sickened to read on, she clicked on the map instead and traced Yonas's long journey to this unlikely place.

A feeling returned—the passive feathered body in her hands. That very day she'd posted the ad for her successor: *The successful applicant will have excellent relationship-building skills.* What cant. Her trouble didn't have to do with her mother. It had to do with her, Marta, and the monstrous phony she was, sashaying through life expecting other people to like her, which, until now, they usually did. Because she had the skills.

ON SATURDAY, JANICE went to pick up Mr Bogdanovic. Marta waved from her front door as she drove off in the truck. And Janice actually lifted her hand off the wheel. Wes stayed behind, shuffling things in the carport, swearing louder than Gorilla's barking.

Marta checked the cake. As she was taking it from the oven, someone knocked at the back door. Wes, in his bandana and a sheepskin jacket that seemed too large, a huge wire dog cage beside him. For transporting the birds, Marta assumed. She'd forgotten the name of the man who owned them now, had no reason to remember it since the arrangements had been turned over to Janice. Mr Bogdanovic was a high school principal beloved even in retirement, or so Marta had gleaned from her subsequent conversations with Janice, each marginally less terse. The bad blood between Janice and Mr Bogdanovic's daughter dated from when Mr B., as everyone called him, moved into the Lodge.

"I'm going to empty the loft," Wes told Marta.

"The what?"

He pointed to what she'd been calling a coop, then scratched his moustache, possibly to hide his smirk. "Here they come."

The approaching truck looked like the advance guard of a tank invasion. Marta couldn't see Mr Bogdanovic until it pulled up on the grass next to her car. Despite a full head of hair, much of it still dark, she placed him in his late seventies. High cheekbones, an aristocratic nose. No mask. Of course,

Marta's wave went unacknowledged. When Janice got out of the truck, Mr Bogdanovic undid his belt and just sat there, staring straight ahead, the picture of aloofness.

What had Marta expected? Gratitude? She waited while Janice opened the passenger door and, with Wes at her side, helped Mr Bogdanovic out of the truck, Wes positioning each foot on the running board. The old man wore a dark wool car coat and beige sneakers with Velcro fasteners. Though he was tall and as vigorous-seeming as his voice on the phone, Janice took his arm and led him toward the still unacknowledged Marta.

He was blind, Marta realized then. She stepped quickly forward. "Mr Bogdanovic? I'm Marta."

His face lit up and his free arm, the one Janice wasn't leading him by, his left, reached out. An awkward clasp. They'd forgotten how to shake hands!

Mr Bogdanovic turned his head toward the Crayola house and made a clicking sound. Immediately, four birds lifted and circled before landing on him. One settled on each hand, one on his shoulder, one on the top of his head. He was beaming now, they all were. He raised the left hand and that bird flew. The pink legs of the right-hand one he slid between his fingers, forming a gentle clasp. He stroked the burbling creature against his cheek.

"This is Rosie," he said, but how could he tell?

He threw Rosie in the air. The other two birds lifted off him as Janice led him to the chairs Marta had set up.

Immediately, Mr Bogdanovic began to question Marta. When had they arrived?

"A week ago." She glanced at Wes emptying the coop. The *loft*. Cat carrier, paint, cardboard boxes—all moved onto the grass.

"Do you know what time?"

"I do," Marta said. "It was about six thirty in the morning. Dawn."

"See?" Mr Bogdanovic told Janice, standing by his side. "Sitting around hasn't slowed them."

"Mr B. did the calculations," Janice explained.

It turned out there'd been a fire on Claude Pettit's farm. Before Marta could react, Wes called, "Okay!" and Mr Bogdanovic reached out his big hand for Janice to take. Marta, who still had no idea what was going on, followed them to the loft. Mr Bogdanovic ducked his head going in. All the birds took wing at once, shit and feathers raining down. They flapped or strutted their way inside. Wes positioned the cage by the door and helped guide Mr Bogdanovic's hands while he loaded the birds.

"Where are you taking them?" Marta asked.

Janice named a park. They were going to release them, then drive back.

"When I call Mr B., you start the timer," she told Marta.

Janice returned Mr Bogdanovic to his chair. She brushed a feather off his shoulder. "We're heading out now, Mr B." For the first time Marta saw her smile.

After they left, Marta brought out coffee and cake, handing each separately to the old man. He rested the plate in his lap.

"How long is it going to take?" she asked.

"Twenty minutes to drive, about the same to fly back."

"They're going to fly as fast as the truck?"

"Might be faster. Except they've been sitting around for so long. Like me."

The years of disease had been toughest on the elderly. Marta was almost grateful that her parents hadn't lived to be, like so many, imprisoned in their rooms. She remembered Yonas then, texted him, and took a chair herself, feeling free to scrutinize Mr Bogdanovic, who was magnificent, forthright like her father, who'd been a union steward.

"How long have you known Janice?" she asked.

"Her whole life." He bit into the cake and, brushing at unseen crumbs, muttered something about barking.

"You mean Gorilla?"

"What? No. I said she's all bark." Just then Gorilla did let loose and they both laughed. "She has quite a story," he said.

"I bet you do too," Marta quipped.

"Yes! I'll tell it to you next time. You'll be sorry."

She felt herself blush with pleasure. Too bad he couldn't see it.

"What about the birds?" she asked. "Where are they going next?"

He gestured toward the loft. "I guess somebody tore off the damn aviary. Wes is going to fix it."

"They're staying?" Marta sputtered. "Mr Bogdanovic? This the first I've heard of it."

He turned his head and fixed her with a magisterial expression.

"I'm not necessarily saying no," she hurried to add.

Just then Yonas arrived with three kids from the center— beltless Brandon, an older youth, who was coatless, and a girl with stick legs. They immediately cleaned her out of cake. It felt crowded now, festive, the kids joshing with Yonas and each other, questioning Mr Bogdanovic about the birds. How had it happened that her yard had suddenly filled with people, her life with birds?

Mr B. told them some of their names—Ivan and Bruce

Willis, Daisy and Rosie. He explained how to read the bands. Brandon waved his hand in front of the old man's face.

"I felt that," Mr Bogdanovic said in principal mode, and the kids all laughed.

"Should I make more coffee?" Marta asked.

Mr Bogdanovic's phone rang in his coat pocket and everyone fell silent. He asked one of the kids to answer. The boy in the T-shirt, who'd been recruited as timer, pressed start.

"What direction should we be looking in?" Yonas asked.

Mr Bogdanovic pointed over his shoulder and Marta oriented herself toward the blue. Little cloud puffs blew around in it like litter. Shortly, the stick-legged girl shouted that she saw one, but it was a false alarm, just some random feathered thing making its way in the world. Marta would have liked to fetch her binoculars—she also needed to pee—but she didn't want to miss anything.

After what seemed like at least a half hour, the young ones pointed. "Look! Over there!"

Marta couldn't see anything, not until the bird was practically in her face, teetering in its descent to the loft. Everyone cheered. A second lone bird arrived a minute later. Only when a group appeared could she properly make them out. Breathlessly, she began describing what she was seeing, for the benefit of the blind man.

"About ten of them now. They're all in a bunch…"

He raised a hand, silencing her, for their advent came, too, with sound. They thrummed, swished. It defied play-by-play anyway, the shape they made in their approach, elongating, then contracting, their distance from each other, mutable as it was, guiding them in.

YOLKI-PALKI

FIRST, A TICKLE—NOT in his throat but the red bag of his lung. It became less playful as the months wore on, more like a taunting prod from a sharp stick. If he didn't exert himself, it let him be, so Varlam just sat there, something he excelled at from his years tending his mother's stall. He began to breathe in a deliberate way too, to surprising effect.

In.

Out.

Certain compromising thoughts, formerly his bane, simply vanished when he focused on his breathing. He was almost happy.

Then, three days ago, he coughed on the bathroom mirror. His reflection stared back, brutish and crimson-spattered. The summer had been hot with fires, the sun a blurry, rose-gold disc travelling through an apocalyptic sky. Smoke was the likely cause of Varlam's troubles, but the doctor, confused about the blood, ordered X-rays anyway.

Now Varlam sat in the room for waiting. Buttocks planted on the hard plastic chair, feet on the disinfected floor, a magazine from the stack on the table open in his lap. When he raised his hand to stifle another cough, the magazine slid. Just in time, Varlam caught it.

He noticed the photograph then. It showed a forest clearing, the larger trees forming a ring around newer, brighter growth. Strangely, he thought he recognized the place. Hadn't Varlam been in that forest as a child? A small boy in city shoes trudging behind a winter-haired woman. Yes, he remembered batting mosquitoes as he took his miserable, left-footed missteps. The woman had seemed so ancient to him, a hundred maybe, despite her vigour, that he was afraid she might fall down dead. He must have believed old people died like that, like cars running out of gas. It had been a long time now since Varlam had believed in anything.

She glanced over her shoulder and, taking pity on him, fished two papirosas from her satchel, and a match, which she struck with a blackened thumbnail. She pinched one of the cardboard tubes and handed it to him—four years old, five at most! Varlam's mother smoked. He knew what to do. Suck, hold, blow. Cough. With the first tarry whiff, the mosquitoes dispersed. There, standing on that green path, Varlam heard a nightingale for the first time. *Life is cruel, cruel, cruel*...The song dizzied him, or the cigarette did.

Someone called the name he was answering to. A lemon-shaped technician in yellow scrubs. He rose and followed her.

In the cubicle, he unbuttoned and removed his shirt. The hairy swell of his stomach filled the cramped space as he struggled with the gown. At last he stepped out with only the nape tie fastened. All the way to the X-ray room, he felt cold air on his back.

The technician directed him to stand before the screen, which she raised up, up, up to the level of his chest by pressing a button on the floor with the toe of her sneaker. The other part of the machine—half camera, half vacuum cleaner—was behind him. Varlam stared at the wall.

He'd been sent to this country almost a year ago, to a supposedly temperate part of it—the Pacific Northwest. A rainforest, though there'd been none of it this summer. Yesterday, the call finally came. When he explained that he didn't feel well, he got dead air in response. It was the first time that Varlam had ever balked and he had to wonder now if there would be consequences. Would he be recalled? Or worse?

The technician scurried to the safety of her booth. "Take a deep breath."

In the second before the cough seized him, he imagined himself shot from behind.

THE DAY AFTER the X-ray he woke to the same muzzy sky. The pinkish eye that portended doom he took personally now.

But there was only one tense moment on the outbound trip, in Security at Sea-Tac, as he nestled his shoes in the tray next to the coiled brown snake of his belt. The stick jabbed his lung and he winced. Just then, the guard looked up from scanning his boarding pass and her glance, brown-eyed and hooded, prolonged to scrutiny. In the end, all she did was ask, "You okay?"

Nodding, Varlam proceeded toward the metal detector.

The old woman was with him still. Memory had pushed her

through the smokescreen of the past and offered up a face. In addition to white hair mannishly cut, there was the diluted blue of her eyes under still-dark brows. No mouth yet. When it arrived, would she speak? He'd been carrying a satchel too— awkwardly. What was in it? Nothing heavy. The strap was too long. The bag kept bumping against his thighs as he walked.

He'd spent a summer with her, he remembered now, but had never returned to visit. The only person who could identify her would be his mother who, presumably, had sent him to the old woman. If he tried to contact her, would she tell him who she was? His mother specialized in withholding desperately sought information. Also in shovelling out the unasked-for shit of her opinions. Besides, she might be dead by now, or just gone from their cement nest. He'd heard they were tearing down those buildings. It pleased Varlam to think of the infernal noise, the exhaust of the machines and the dust, as they efficiently pulverized the place.

He bought a black coffee and went to wait at his gate.

High in the corner, a silent TV broadcast the grander pain of the world.

HE FLEW SOUTH in a commuter plane that, two and a half hours later, descended to a kind of Mars: cinnamon corrugations of mountains swathed in brown cloud. A treeless, low-rise city spreading like rash. He emerged, stiff and cramped, as though out of a can. Then a pore-flooding walk to the terminal, Varlam coughing painfully the whole way. His left testicle glued itself to his inner thigh. He shook it off his leg.

But there *were* trees, just not along the highway, or on the city's franchised fringes. As the cab approached downtown, they suddenly appeared, struggling on the parched verges, leaves gasping, cuffed at their bases in grey plastic mesh. Three or four per block, they seemed immature, barely saplings, which made Varlam wonder. Had some disease wiped out their predecessors?

At that moment the long-ago satchel opened to him and, with his surprised inhalation, the stick thrust, so punishingly this time that he had to curl around the pain and press his forehead against the headrest in front of him. After a few moments, when he was finally able to straighten, he saw the round, brown face of the driver looking back at him in fright.

"You need a doctor?"

Varlam shook his head.

They pulled up in front of the hotel, into the shade of a grossly out-of-proportion porte-cochère. One foot on the ground, then the other, Varlam eased himself into the heat.

He was still marvelling over the satchel's contents, but as the hotel doors slid open, he remembered the call that had summoned him here, and the intimidating silence that had gathered around his excuse. Varlam was already living under the name of a dead man. He scanned the lobby. But if something was going to happen to him, wouldn't it happen *after* he completed the job?

Forms, credit card imprint—the dead man's name on everything. He kept his head down.

"And one more thing, sir." A manila envelope slid across the counter.

In his room, dim from the blackout drapes, he tossed the envelope and his bag on one of the beds. Sitting on the other, he slipped off his shoes then lay back, closing his eyes. Now he could unload the satchel. Inside—the very thing he'd imagined prodding him. Sticks! The old woman made them by tap-tapping slivers from a log, he remembered now. She wouldn't let him touch the axe, but when she had a pile of sticks, she showed him how to play spillikins so he could amuse himself while she went about her work. He gathered them into a bundle, let go. They fell all higgledy-piggledy. The point was to lift them one by one out of the jumbled pile without disturbing the rest.

She set a rusted can on the ground, opened it with a twist of her knife. Varlam scooched closer, raking the pile of sticks along. He took one, stirred the paint, then let the drips fall back into the can. When the dripping stopped, he left them to dry, planting the unpainted end in the ground.

Was he dreaming those small hands smeared red? Dreaming her wiping them with her sour rag? He must have slept because, when his eyes opened, the semi-darkness confused him. He rolled off the bed and, tripping over his shoes, went to the window where he parted the heavy drapes just enough to see down into a courtyard. A man in coveralls and a baseball cap was circling the pool, trailing a net. If Varlam had slept, it couldn't have been for more than a few minutes.

In the light from the slit, he opened the envelope. The next day's plane ticket, the hotel confirmation, a flip phone, a business card, cash. The card and bills went into his wallet, the phone his pocket. He dropped the envelope on the bed and retrieved his toiletry case from his bag.

He couldn't say that the face he splashed with water now was any different than the one he'd spattered with blood four days before. Same wide rubbery mouth and drooping eyes. A five-o'clock shadow by noon. His hair grew so thickly the clippers couldn't get near his scalp. It was beginning to tuft from his ears too. He'd been vaguely proud of this vigour, but only because what else was there? But now he'd retrieved this memory. He'd pulled it from the bottom, causing everything to shift.

He and the old woman had been planting trees.

THE NEXT CAB took him to a strip mall fifteen minutes away, where Varlam stood blinking through the sting of sweat. A liquor outlet with a sheet of plywood over one window, an Indian restaurant strung with what looked like tinsel. Nail salon, dog groomer, dry cleaner. Usually, it was a travel agent or a tax office. He checked the card again. The groomer.

As he entered, the smell assailed him. Wet dog, shampoo. Ahead was a counter and, in the tiled area beyond it, a plump woman in a patterned smock bathing a brown dog. Strands of hair from her unkempt knot hung in her eyes. She kept blowing at them as she scrubbed.

"You here for Andy?" she called to Varlam.

"Andy!" she yelled.

The dog scrambled to get out of the tub, but she grabbed his collar and soothed him with clicking sounds. "That's a good boy, who's going to be pretty, who's a pretty boy?"

The dog settled with a look of infinite patience.

The dogs of Varlam's childhood were not pretty. Motley gangs of them had roamed the birdless no man's land between the apartment blocks. Size was irrelevant. The ankle-high ones could be the most savage. Once he found a litter of puppies secreted in the weeds. He picked one up, thinking he'd bring the squirming thing home as a pet. Then he saw that it was crawling with fleas, that they were drinking from the puppy's scabbed eyes. He dropped it and ran, which was just as well. She would have drowned it in the toilet.

"Good boy, pretty boy," the woman cooed. "Knock," she told Varlam, pointing.

Between a pair of metal shelves stocked with supplies was a door plastered with pin-ups of show dogs. He went over and knocked.

A man's voice called, "Yeah?"

Varlam looked inside. Judging by the cardboard boxes stacked everywhere, the office doubled as a storage area. The man, Andy, was thumbing his phone with his feet up on a crowded desk. When he saw Varlam, the scuffed brown shoes swung to the floor. His eyes, lazy with indifference a second ago, began jumping in their sockets.

"Pickup?"

He opened the bottom drawer of the desk and took out a stuffed toy—a tan rabbit with black stitching for its eyes and nose. Half rising from his chair, he stretched out his arm to hand it to Varlam, who usually dealt in padded envelopes. Dead air filled Varlam's ears again.

"Is something wrong?" the man asked.

Varlam took the rabbit and closed the door behind him.

The woman was vigorously towelling the dog now. As Varlam left, she sang out a sunny, "Bye!"

It rained dust here, he observed as he waited for the next cab. The cars—the few in the parking lot and the ones driving past on the road—were matte with it. And the supposed rainforest where Varlam had been living was on fire. Even someone like him who paid no attention to the news—the recounting of the day's calamities, the toll of its dead—recognized the coming end. From now on, it would be a slow, deluded trudge toward the finish. Nevertheless, he and the old woman had persisted.

She had a complete face now, determined, yet merry, with wiry hairs like bent pins jutting from her chin. He'd wanted to touch them, to test their stiffness, but of course didn't. This was during the long evenings when they sat in her cottage sipping the concoction that she brewed. If his serving came from the bottom of the jar, he might get lucky. It might include a bloated raisin, which he'd hold in the cup of his tongue, slowly pressing it against his palate until it finally popped and its sweetness flooded his mouth.

There was a trunk too, containing huge creaking boots, a brown leather belt with a pouch, and a watch face without a strap. She let him play with these things, even stomp around in the thigh-high boots, because, in time, they would be his, she said. So she must have been his grandmother. Then why was he never sent to her again?

Also in the trunk—old books, and a ledger that she consulted after each forest visit. He couldn't yet read, but he remembered that the ink had faded to the colour of her eyes. The sticks they'd collected that day lay on the table, one or two broken by wandering animals or falling branches, a few merely weathered. She got him to count them. Maybe she taught him to count using those sticks. The broken ones she tossed in the stove. The still-usable ones she cleaned with her rag.

For every tree they planted, there was a stick to accompany it. She noted in the ledger how many they would have to replant. There always had to be a certain number. Back then, he understood this without her saying so.

Couldn't a hiker have tripped on a stick and broken it?

Varlam wondered this now. Or maybe the village children had sabotaged their project. They spat at Varlam and the old woman when they walked down the road with their satchels, sometimes even pelted them with rocks. The adults merely turned their backs.

They never ran into anyone up there in the forest. Never.

The cab appeared then, its logo nearly erased by grit. It turned off the road a little too fast, skidding as it pulled up in front of Varlam.

Two hundred and sixty-three, he remembered as he compacted himself into the chilled backseat. Two hundred and sixty-three pine saplings grew in that clearing.

The driver, white with a stringy ponytail, smirked in the rear-view mirror. When Varlam noticed, he tensed up.

"Where to?" the man asked, and in his gaze, Varlam suddenly saw his own ludicrousness—a man so huge that his head grazed the ceiling, a toy rabbit in his lap.

He named his hotel.

What did the rabbit mean? Why conceal it in a toy when, until now, a padded envelope sufficed? At the very least, the guy could have put the rabbit in a bag.

The situation got even more comical as, gazing straight ahead, he began discreetly palpating the rabbit, as he should have done in the office, to make sure it was there. If the driver happened to glance in the rear-view mirror again, he'd think that Varlam was adjusting himself, or worse.

Finally, his fingers detected something buried in its belly. He squeezed. With the sudden loud squeak, both men startled.

For the rest of the ride, Varlam coughed.

*

USUALLY, HE ORDERED room service. He'd especially wanted to today so he could remember in peace while he ate, but when he sat at the desk, he discovered that the kneehole wouldn't accommodate his legs. Twisted sideways, he used the corkscrew to unpick the seams of the rabbit's head. There was the atomizer, tucked inside like an evil brain.

At the entrance to the restaurant, a beige-carpeted expanse that overlooked the courtyard, the hostess asked, "Reservation? No problem! One?"

She stepped out from behind her podium with the laminated menu in hand. Varlam followed her hips in their tight black skirt to a table overlooking the pool, which he refused, pointing instead to one in the corner with a view of the entire restaurant and bar.

The bar was where everyone had gathered now for happy hour. Seated, Varlam glanced over at them, the same sort of business travellers as everywhere—men in jackets and loosened ties, always more men than women, the latter giving off a certain brassy air, tinged with a desperation that he put down to divorce.

His server appeared in his peripheral vision. "Anything to drink?"

Varlam declined with a wave. He drank when he finished the job. She filled his water glass, ice plopping, while he scanned the menu for recognizable items.

After he ordered, he turned toward the window. The courtyard plants looked lush and shiny—plastic?—but the palms were shedding brown fronds into the pool. He thought of the long walk into the cool shade of pines, the sweet odour of running sap, the fairy tale–ness of it. Maybe it never happened. But he couldn't deny these evanescing memories. Hints, or clues, they had to have some connection to his present situation—the burden of his work, the issue with his lungs. Why else would a magazine picture trigger such a reappraisal, if that was what this was? Yet he couldn't quite believe, either, that he'd been doing something good.

The server, still un-looked at, returned with his soup and a basket of rolls. Tomato. He saw the rusted can, the lid popping off with the twist of the knife.

He remembered plenty, of course, that he was using to stuff the holes. Earlier, he'd remembered the dogs, a definite fact. His mother's stall in the market, where she'd sold hardware and household goods. Lengths of rope, extension cords, work gloves, light bulbs, batteries, tape, saws, doormats, dishtowels. For these banal items, his memory was photographic. The rope was bundled in different lengths according to type. He even remembered the prices! As soon as she trusted him to count the money correctly, he was often left in charge, sometimes for what seemed like hours. *Where did you go?* That earned him a clack on the side of his head.

In the bar, they let out a cheer over some game on TV. He squinted. Basketball.

Soup finished, he tore a roll in half and used it to swab the bowl.

There must have been a man. His mother must have sent Varlam away so that she could be with him. But who would want a whore, especially one saddled with a child? No one, apparently, because Varlam came back. She seemed shrunken then, defeated. For many months she wore a kerchief like an old woman. When she finally took it off, he saw that she'd shorn her head.

The people in the bar were all rising to their feet. Some

shook hands while others began migrating in Varlam's direction, carrying unfinished drinks. Varlam watched from the corner of his eye as two women teetered toward the table diagonal to his. In their early forties, they dressed like twenty with long streaky hair, short skirts, and high heels. The taller one sat with her back to Varlam. The short one—she wore ankle boots with open toes—took her time, first setting down her wineglass, then slinging the chain of her bag over the back of the chair, then flipping the mess of her hair off her broad shoulders. She had a stocky, full-breasted torso barely buttoned into a bright floral blouse, and legs as skinny as a hen's.

Varlam faced the window again. That was when the old woman finally spoke. "Yolki-palki," she said. It was an expression he hadn't heard in years. She'd used it when her match wouldn't strike, or the paint dripped on his bare legs, or he tripped on the path and fell flat on his face.

"Yolki-palki!"

There was something else too. Something she'd said numerous times, as though reciting lines in a play. "The people who come a hundred years, or a couple of hundred years after us? They'll despise us for having lived so stupidly. Perhaps they'll find a way to be happy. As for us? There's only one hope for you and me. The hope that when we're sleeping in our graves we may see visions—nice ones."

His steak appeared then, fries taking up half the plate. A spillikins of fries! He pulled one out from the bottom, causing several to slide onto the tablecloth.

"I'll be back with the ketchup," the server said.

Unappetizing, the steak's dinge between the darker stripes from the grill. His whole past was in that colour, with the exception of the forest. The identical apartment blocks, the drab clothes, the boiled food. If there'd been any meat on his plate then, it would have been in the form of gristly chunks. Yet when he cut into the steak now, it bled in colour. Here he sat on the other side of the world eating anything he wanted. Nice apartment in a place that, when it wasn't on fire, was clean and safe. What a vision that would have seemed to him back then!

What people had she been talking about? he wondered.

The ketchup bottle thunked down. From the women's table came a burst of cackling. Though he kept his eyes on his plate, he knew that they were leaning toward each other in that conspiratorial manner of women.

In two hundred years? Would there be any people left when all the trees were gone?

With that thought, he was impaled. He dropped his cutlery to grab the table's edge. Doused in sweat, afraid of blacking out, he forced open his eyes only to have them roll in their sockets. Had they poisoned him?

In the distance, some kind of commotion—squawking, a flurry of movement. A hand shook him. Sour, wine-tinged breath, some chemical fug he barely recognized as perfume.

"Is he okay?" the server asked.

The pain subsided. So grateful for this reprieve, Varlam looked fully into the face of the woman crouching at his side, whose small hand with its rings and bright, glued-on nails weighed as much as a songbird perched on his shoulder. Plucked brows sunk low, hazel eyes circled in crayon. Below her face, an unfathomable cleft strung with gold chains.

"I'm fine." He was shivering, nauseated.

"Honey, you sure?"

He picked up his fork again to prove it and, under her doubtful gaze, stuffed in a fry.

"Okay." She let him go and, rising out of her crouch, pointed over to where the tall woman had swivelled around in her chair to stare at them. The tall one was prettier, he saw now, and younger. Up close, this one might even have been Varlam's age under all her paint.

"You want to join us?"

"No, thank you," he told her.

"Okay. You can change your mind, right?"

She flashed a fluorescent smile, then went back to her place. As he picked his way through his meal, Varlam sensed her glancing over from time to time.

The server returned to take away his plate and offer dessert. He wasn't ready to try standing. Coffee, pie.

What time was it? He patted his pocket, then remembered he'd left the flip phone in his room. His own phone was on the counter where he lived, awaiting his return. He imagined tapping to unlock the X-ray results, grey rungs arching on either side of his bleached spine, a translucent cage around the thing growing there. He could feel some part of it tickling, another part boring in.

They wouldn't send the X-rays. He would have to make an appointment.

The pie came—sweetened glue in a crust. He pushed it away and drank the coffee in tiny, bitter sips, while the brown sky above the sickened palms deepened to black. He focused on his breathing.

In.

Out.

Diners came and went. The women, too, were gone by the time he signed the check.

*

SHE WAS IN the lobby, standing by the elevator, like a busty little tank on short stilts. The hair on the back of Varlam's neck, the hair all over his back, reared. He retreated a step.

She turned her head. "Oh, hi! Going up?"

She stabbed at the button with her painted nail. Many bracelets clinked.

Varlam glanced across the lobby to the front doors. He could step out to get some air. Air that would be like a plastic bag pulled over his head. The vomitty sensation returned. Who was she? Had they sent her?

When the elevator opened, he let her go in first. The top of her head, with its blond streaks, was level with his sternum. She had to lean back on the heels of her boots to look into his face.

"What floor?"

"Three," Varlam said.

"Same as me!" The painted nail stabbed again. "Where're you from?"

"Boston." It was the first far place that came to mind.

She snorted. "I meant before. Anyway, you can probably tell from *my* accent that I'm from Texas, but I live in Denver now. The whole office's down here for a big conference. I'm in packaging solutions. What do you do?"

"Forestry."

The seedlings grew behind the cottage, their feathery needles bright and soft, the long fibrous taproots covered in dirt-clumped hairs. The elevator rose. The old woman scooped them out of the ground with her bare hand, tenderly cupping them as she transferred them to her satchel. Then they began their long walk to the forest.

The doors chimed and opened. They stepped into the beige of the hallway. Varlam paused, waiting for her to go first, so he could go in the opposite direction, though that would mean turning his back.

"Listen," the woman said. "Back in the restaurant? I thought you were having a heart attack. You scared the bejesus out of me! I know this sounds like I'm making a pass at you or something, but I assure you I am not. I'm a trained Healing Touch Practitioner. Do you know what that is? Honey, at dinner? I couldn't hardly eat for thinking how badly you need my help."

Varlam looked down on her stiff little form tilted back, nose crinkling as she waited for a response.

"The name's a bit misleading because I actually won't touch you."

He almost laughed because it seemed perfectly obvious now that she was a hooker.

"How much?" he asked.

"Oh!" Her crayoned eyes widened. "Oh, my goodness! No! I wouldn't charge you. Some people charge because it's their profession, but I don't. For me, it's a *calling*. I just want to take your pain away. You're in pain, aren't you?"

The question startled him. His mouth opened, but his tongue felt too fat to shape itself into a denial.

"Good. Let's go to your room. I have about a thousand samples spread around mine."

Varlam began to walk and, though he knew the way, he felt disoriented with her trotting along beside him. When they reached his door, he had to pat himself down for the key card. He tapped and held open the door. She scurried into the darkness.

"I'm Darlene, by the way," she called.

She found the light switch, which simultaneously illuminated the bedside lamp and the one on the desk, where she deposited her handbag with its clattering chain. Varlam let the door sigh closed. She bent to unzip her boots. Kicking them off brought her even closer to the floor. He wasn't convinced of her non-whoreness. What kind of name was Darling? Meanwhile, she was wriggling her hands out of her bangles and tucking them in her bag, rings too, then the chains that draped her chest.

"The metal interferes with the energy," she said, glancing over at him. "Go on. Have a seat."

Varlam sat on the end of the closer bed.

"Aw!" She snatched the rabbit off the desk and held it right up to her face, pressing her nose to the embroidered one. The corkscrew from the mini-bar lay there somewhere. "What a cutie patootie!"

Whatever expression took control of his face, it caused her to put the rabbit down in a hurry and begin rooting through her jewellery-swallowing handbag. She found a hair elastic and in three deft flicks contained her streaky mass. Barefoot, she brisked over, insinuating herself in the space between the beds. She patted the facing bed, then boosted herself up.

Varlam came and sat where she'd indicated. They were knee to knee now. Mid-fifties without the distraction of her hair. Around her mouth, he saw pouching. The skin on her neck looked loose. Again, the awful perfume, which could only remind him of the rabbit's poisonous brain. They must have sent her.

She extended her palms as though pressing an invisible wall, all the while fixing him with a strange unseeing gaze. Varlam just sat there like he used to in the market, hunched, ape arms dangling between his legs, eyes darting everywhere but at her.

Eventually he decided that she wanted him to press his hands against hers, but when he lifted them, she said, "Don't move."

He coughed. Winced.

"Okay," she said cheerily. "I got it."

"What?" Varlam asked. Instead of replying, she slithered to the floor and began unlacing his shoes. Next would come the blow job, Varlam assumed.

Instead—"Whoops!"—she gripped his ankles and swung both his feet up and to the side in one strong motion. He found himself supine, staring at the sprinkler on the ceiling, which looked like a miniature blade of a circular saw. Bending her scented cleavage over him, she tugged the pillow free from behind his head so that he flattened on the mattress. Her whole arm slid under his knees and, this way, she managed to lever his legs and jam the pillow under them.

"How's that?" she asked. "Comfortable? Good. We'll get started now. Close your eyes."

She snapped off the bedside light. The one on the desk stayed lit. He could still make out her face and its frown.

"You gotta trust me, honey, for this to work. Close your eyes."

He did and, right away, heard rustling. She was rubbing her hands together.

"So many thoughts!" she exclaimed. "Everything you have to do tomorrow? I want you to give it one last think. Then just leave it all and be in this room with me. Can you do that?"

He nodded.

First, he'd get up early to catch his flight. Another address. It might be a hotel room, an apartment, or a house. Someone would phone and tell him when to go. There was nothing to it. He didn't actually touch anyone. If they told him to, he'd go inside, but usually he didn't. He spritzed the door handle and that delicate mist was apparently enough to kill a person. Then he'd turn the rubber glove inside out, knotting the atomizer inside. And here was another thing he would never have dreamed back in the market: on almost any street anywhere in this country, you can find a trash receptacle.

"Ready?" she asked.

He nodded again. Weight settling more fully on the mattress, he began to breathe.

In.

Out.

"So much pain," she whispered. "It's not your fault. All that shit comes from your parents, and from their parents too. On and on. That's how it works."

Did it? He felt the heat of her palms hovering just above his face.

In.

Out.

Was she real? There was something dwarf-like about her, something sinister in the way she was growing old before his eyes. It seemed far-fetched, as well, that he would allow this to happen. He remembered her touching his shoulder in the restaurant. Did she put a spell on him? *Yolki-palki! Yolki-palki!* Or was this the end of the longer spell of his life, the one that began with him sitting behind the extension cords and light bulbs and the various lengths of rope when a man he knew by sight, but not by name, appeared out of nowhere? Droopy moustache and new-looking clothes. Varlam remembered a particular shirt, red with a wide pointed collar. Where did he get such clothes? He might as well have come strolling through the market dressed in a magician's robe. *She's not here*, Varlam had said. It wasn't his mother he'd come for, but Varlam, the hard-working son who took his blows without complaint, all grown up now. He'd grown and grown and grown into a compliant ogre in a story.

Scum, his mother had said when he told her. *Like your grandfather.*

In.

Out.

Her hands floated above his eyes now. *Yolki-palki. Tree-sticks, fiddlesticks*. She'd come to take him back. He was drowsy. In. Soon he'd fall asleep. Out.

Would he even wake? If he did, where would he be? Trudging home in the cold, stepping over the frozen pool of piss at the building's entrance, climbing the echoing stairs. The paint is still peeling on the concrete walls. Wires buzz on every landing. At the door—he has to bend to enter—he pauses to listen for what sounds she might be making inside, to know how drunk she is.

No. He breathes in the forest. Breathes in the seed that plants itself inside him. For now, though, there is no pain. It will take years to root.

Varlam is very small when the vision opens to him: a clearing filled with scarlet stakes. They look like flowers! And the birds are calling sweetly to each other. He almost doesn't hear the children down in the village, singing too. *Murderer, murderer, murderer* ... Two-hundred and sixty-three people lie asleep there. The old woman tends a tree for every one. *What choice did he have*, she tells him. *Otherwise, he'd be here too. And then where would you be, my child, my precious?*

Precious? She means him! He is precious.

He wants to stay with her, and would, except that, just then, across the clearing, the underbrush rustles and its branches part. He's horrified to see it, repelled. A little brown rabbit, scampering toward him.

STARTED EARLY, TOOK MY DOG

DREW WAS OVER by the climbing dome, swaying as he talked at another child, the dark drape of his hair concealing worried eyes that rarely settled during a conversation—which this definitely wasn't. From several yards away, Ani could hear his voice taking on that irritating squeak.

"Your name isn't real. You don't have a name."

Over and over.

The other boy, a crouching hulk compared to Drew, made busy digging in the wood chips. When he finally answered, his "Yes, I do," came out as a low, exasperated growl. Ani could tell he'd soon cry from sheer vexation. Even Jesus, their rescue dog in all senses of the word, knew it. He kept tugging in the children's direction.

The problem was that Ani was being talked at herself by another mother, one with glasses and lank brown hair. Apparently, there was a birthday party to which all the second graders were invited.

"Unless you think Drew doesn't want to come," the other mother said. "Then I won't bother with the loot bag."

Finally, Ani seized her chance to step away. "I'll go ask him." The dog, wagging, led her straight to Drew, who cried, "Jesus!" and bent stiffly to hug him, but not Ani.

"Your dog has a name," the other boy said, reasonably.

"No," Drew said. "We just call him that."

Meanwhile, Jesus kept on pulling. Pulling hard, and now he let out a strange strangled sound, one that Ani had never heard, and lunged so unexpectedly she had to scramble to keep hold of the leash. He was trying to reach the chain-link fence at the back of the schoolyard, behind which a man stood smoking a cigarette. Grubby red ball cap, baggy jeans, untucked plaid shirt. As soon as Ani saw him, she reinterpreted Jesus's tail. This wasn't wagging; it was slashing.

The man knew he'd been seen, yet all he did was turn sideways so she couldn't make out his face, only a dirty-blond fringe of hair at his nape. He must have been there the whole time, smoking and watching the kids.

Ani dragged Jesus, whining now, back to where the loot bag mother had joined two more, forming a coven, Ani couldn't help thinking. She interrupted their meeting.

"Do you see that guy over there?"

Maternal instincts kicked in. "Who? Where?" They broke open their circle, scanning the schoolyard.

Ani pointed and the stranger dropped his cigarette. If his departure was in any way hurried, it couldn't compare to theirs as they crossed the patchy grass, Jesus dragging Ani, choking himself. Her shoulder socket strained. The dog seemed to want to make friends now, as he usually did, but by the time they reached the fence all that remained for Jesus to greet was half a cigarette still smoldering in the damp earth.

The loot bag mother said, "That was definitely not a parent. I'm on the PAC. I know *everybody*."

THE NEXT MORNING, as Freya got Drew ready for school, Ani lay in bed thinking about her non-encounter with the stranger. Specifically, what had happened in her body—the jolt when she spotted him loitering behind the fence, and how it had sent a pulse singing down every nerve. Her reflex had been the same as all the other mothers: to protect her child. Unambiguous, pure.

Meanwhile, in the kitchen, Freya was encouraging Drew to eat in her soft, eternally patient voice. Her singsong lifted above the clatter.

"Bite the little toast dog before he bites you!"

Freya did things like cookie-cutter the toast. Sometimes it worked. Sometimes Drew would open his mouth while he looked at his book. When Ani was in charge of breakfast, she often had to fight an urge to pry his mouth open.

Yesterday, Ani had asked Drew, "Did you see that man by the fence?"

"There wasn't a man."

"No?"

"There were X chromosomes and Y chromosomes."

"So you did see him?"

No reply.

The door creaked and Ani rolled, pulling the pillow over her head. From under that soft blind, she spied Freya creeping to the dresser. She was probably picking her rings out of the little silver box there and looking at the hump of Ani while she put them on. Maybe she was wondering if Ani was only pretending to be asleep. *Leave*, Ani thought. Her second wifely betrayal in as many days. Yesterday, after the incident, Freya had texted, wondering where they were. *Stayed to play leaving now*, Ani had replied. If Drew mentioned the man, of course she would tell Freya what had happened.

Freya floated off. Soon Ani heard Drew wailing as he was separated from his book. Tooth brushing and dressing seemed to take an hour. Finally, the refrain of keys and the metal screen door, followed by quiet.

Then the sound Ani had been waiting for—the day's delight. A gentle ticking coming down the uncarpeted hall. When it stopped just outside the bedroom, the clock of her heart accelerated. Ani made a tiny kissing sound.

The door flew open, striking the dresser, and Jesus leapt. He leapt onto the bed beside Ani and burrowed down under the covers, deep, where he was absolutely not allowed to be.

EVENTUALLY THEY GOT moving. By then Freya had returned from dropping Drew at school, their silver hybrid parked under the shaggy overhang of cedars in the gravelled area between the house and workshop, along with the car driven by one of her sewists. Another sewist's bike leaned against the workshop wall. Freya designed her own line of sustainable clothing, clothes she wore herself, voluminous and fluttery, that looked best on tall dancer-types like her, or fat women. Ani, being neither, sported the family jeans.

The screen door complained as they went out the back. "*I started Early—Took my Dog—/And visited the Sea*," Ani recited.

There was a sea for them to walk to, or rather the Strait of Georgia. Technically it was an ocean. Was there a difference?

After three years on the Sunshine Coast, she still didn't know. She'd lived most of her life in Toronto, where she'd worked in publishing, and a couple of flailing years in New York—places where "sea" referred to humanity as encountered on a subway platform. They weren't sea-bound today, though. That was the way to town, to Gibsons, where Freya had grown up, famously the setting of an ancient TV series that Ani had never seen. It, the town, sat at the bottom of the long, long hill, overlooking a dollopy array of islands.

Instead, after Ani and the dog had walked the length of the drive, passing the vegetable garden at the front of the house, they turned in the opposite direction. Along this way, the occasional roadside stall offered honey or fresh eggs from battered picnic coolers, it being too early in the season for produce. Birds flew back and forth bearing stereotypic tufts of grass or twigs. Drivers passing would see Ani—a diminutive woman in her forties, dark hair in a short, angular cut, stride athletic—and think she was walking alone, so wide was the circle that Jesus trotted. He was herding her, behaviour that, along with his erect feathered ears and a feather-duster tail, suggested at least some border collie in the mixed bag of him. She didn't worry about cars; if he looped too far onto the road, she only had to whistle to bring him back. And despite not entirely trusting the locals, she conceded that they were courteous, swerving to make space, always lifting the fingers of one hand off the wheel in a semi-wave.

Jesus disappeared into the birdsongy trees and Ani fell into thought, this morning about the poem. It had popped into her head a few days ago from wherever it had been secreting itself since her university days. She'd immediately made a ritual of reciting that first line, but only now did she find herself reflecting on Dickinson herself. So odd! When the family had guests, she'd conceal herself behind the parlour door, or simply keep to her room. For the last twenty years of her life, she never left the house at all. Seclusion in exchange for a secret, outrageous productivity.

Ani was huffing a little now, nylon jacket sleeves swishing. Was remembering the poem an unconscious rebuke? She was an adherent of solitude, too, yet had achieved absolutely nothing since coming here. She could have freelanced as an editor but hadn't reached out.

A truck rattled toward them. Ani whistled and Jesus, reappearing, fell into position at her heel. Almost immediately, she heard crunching from behind. The truck had stopped. An older model, a lustreless red and white with a chrome bumper. It drove right on.

And then—I started—too— Ani walking with the dog and poem, until they reached the six-foot stump chainsawed into the shape of a rearing bear at the end of someone's drive, at which point this frightful kitsch forced them back.

It was only then, on their return, that the poem unexpectedly burst—an aneurysm of meaning. Because, in it, there was a He, just like there'd been at the school the day before, the Sea, rearing menacingly, chasing the narrator all the way to town. There, where witnesses abounded, He feigned gallantry and withdrew, *With a Mighty look— / At me—*. Ani remembered, too, that long-ago seminar when the women around the table had agreed on the meaning of that *Mighty look*. There'd been a series of sexual assaults on campus that semester and the university had organized a safe-walk program. Yet the men—boys really—had scoffed at their interpretation, while the professor—cardiganed, geriatric—had merely twitched his lips.

*

BACK HOME, ANI riffed in her journal about uselessness. Why not go back to copyediting and pick up a contract or two? This quickly morphed into self-defence. Freya, after all, had never so much as hinted that Ani get a job, despite the fact that they could have used the money. She understood that at this stage of their lives, or Drew's, Ani lacked the mental space. Until she got back from her long walk with Jesus, she was good for nothing. If not for the dog, she probably wouldn't get out of bed.

Jesus had been something of a plot twist in her life, like marriage and motherhood. Though decidedly not a Dog Person, Ani found that she loved this particular dog and their uncomplicated relationship. Whistle, he came. Throw the ball, he returned it. Lie sobbing on the bed, he was there to drink her tears. Jesus was her respite—from the constant effort of managing her own behaviours so as not to set off undesirable ones in her child, and from Drew's hundred daily rejections of her. Freya, of course, didn't feel rejected. She felt "differently loved."

The poem had set this thought train in motion. Ani looked it up now and copied it in her finger-cramping semi-cursive.

And He—He followed—close behind—

She thought of the schoolyard loiterer again. How coolly he'd turned his shoulder. He didn't care that Ani had seen him. The reaction of the other mothers had confirmed her sense of menace. Normally, Ani felt disconnected from those women, even threatened by them, but the truth was that if anyone wanted to hurt the children, or them—*He would eat me up*—it would be a man.

Then laundry and internet surfing. She lost the day again and had to rush to pick up Drew.

Only a few minutes late, she found him standing alone in the playground, hugging his turtle backpack. Her heart was the thing that cramped now, seeing him as others must, as thin and anxious, waiflike despite receiving twice the industry standard of mothering.

"Sorry I'm a little late, sweetie."

"Did you bring my book?" He looked crushed when she told him no.

"Let's go," she said cheerily, but just then the loot bag mother approached. Because of the commotion yesterday, she never got an answer about the birthday party.

"Does he want to come?"

Ani glanced at the fence. No one there, though Jesus's amber eyes were riveted exactly where the man had been. He remembered him too. The stranger's presence had briefly united Ani with this other mother, whose name she hadn't bothered to learn, and whose awkwardness around Drew now brought out the porcupine in Ani.

Frequently, Ani had to model appropriate behaviours for her son, but this time she performed the service for the other mother. "Drew? I think this woman wants to ask you something."

Because of Ani's tone, or her scalding expression, the other mother blushed. "Do you want to come to Tyson's party, Drew?" she asked, almost in falsetto.

No reply.

Immediately, Ani realized her error. She'd have to get a reply out of him in order to prove her point, but that required her to act out a deeply private struggle. She squatted face-to-face with Drew and, enclosing his slender wrist, squeezed.

"Sweetheart, do you want to go to the party?"

He twisted his whole body away. Jesus immediately tucked himself tight against Drew's leg. When Drew finally shook his head, Ani yearned to pull her strange son to her chest and hold him. The fact that she couldn't was excruciating. Sensing this too, Jesus stretched out his neck to lick her face.

Ani stood and told the woman, "There's your answer." She walked off with Jesus, Drew trailing them.

"You!" Drew called from behind.

Ani stopped beside the car and took a calming breath. "Are you talking to me?"

He caught up, dragging the turtle by its strap. "Why didn't you remember my book?"

"Don't call me 'You.' Call me 'Mom,' or 'Ani,' or 'Anika.' 'You' isn't nice."

She opened the rear door. Drew clambered into his booster seat and Jesus leapt in beside him. "But you're not my mom. You're chromosomes."

"Actually, I *am* your mother." Ani slammed the door and got in the front.

She drove clenching the wheel. "You're not," Drew kept saying from the back seat. "Ani, you're chromosomes. You are. You are." If she didn't concede, his desperate voice would keep climbing the register until it was a drill in her ear.

"Remember how we talked about this? You made a point. I heard you. Now it's better to stop talking about it."

"But you are!"

"Okay, I am. I am only chromosomes. You are one hundred percent correct, as usual."

She glanced at him in the rear-view mirror, leaning his head against the window, eyes closed. As exhausted as she was.

At home, while Drew ran to fetch his book, she unpacked his uneaten lunch, arranging Freya's perfect sandwich triangles on a plate just in case. With Drew installed in the corner of her office, textbook open in his lap, plate balanced on the arm of the chair, she returned to her desk. Jesus flopped onto his side on the rag rug.

Through the window, Ani saw that the sewists were leaving for the day. Freya stood in the open door of the workshop speaking to the older one with frizzy hair—they'd gone to high school together—while the two younger ones who ride-shared waited in the car. The fourth was preparing to mount her bike. A trainee hired through a program for at-risk youth, she affected a feral look, hair seemingly rinsed with India ink. Throughout the day she snuck out for text-and-smoke breaks. If Ani and Jesus happened to be outside, Jesus would peel from Ani's side and run to greet her.

Now the girl wobbled the bike down the gravelled drive past the window where Ani, utterly wretched, sat. Her eyes lifted. Crudely circled with kohl, they were a pretty, un-Goth aquamarine. Seeing Ani watching her, she dropped them the way Drew always did.

ON A ROAD of mostly split-levels, their bungalow stood out for its dilapidated charms: wood-shingled with leaded-glass windows, rambling vegetable garden. On Saturday, with Drew reading on the steps and Jesus crouching nearby waiting for someone to throw the mould-coloured tennis ball, Ani and Freya worked. Each shovelful Ani turned seethed with worms.

Freya was harvesting the winter kale. Apropos of nothing, she came over, wiped Ani's cheek with her sleeve, then kissed her. Kissed her mouth and with one flick of Freya's tongue against hers, an exquisite charge radiated out of Ani's cunt.

"Mud?" Ani asked, and Freya said yes. But she'd also just

wanted to kiss her. She stooped for the ball and threw it. Jesus tore off.

This was how Freya had tackled Ani's noncommittal heart in the first place a decade ago, with a casual approach. The bodycheck followed. She'd pinned her down until Ani had cried out, *yes, yes, yes!* And now Freya only had to repeat this formula to shake Ani out of her darker moods.

But then a sound insinuated itself, a particular rattle. Almost before Ani had consciously identified the sound as an engine—the one belonging to the truck from yesterday, that had stopped in the middle of the road—her grip on the shovel released. She found herself racing across the sodden garden nearly as fast as Jesus was returning with the slimed ball.

She slipped, landing in the black mud. Scrambled to her feet. Kept running all the way to the drainage ditch that ran along the road, which she leapt. Now she was right behind the chrome bumper, running hard, but flagging. CHEVRO-LET filled its tailgate.

"Fuck you!" she screamed. "Leave us the fuck alone!"

Jesus reached her first. Bent double on the road, Ani was trying to catch her breath, hands bracing her thighs, one wearing a glove of mud. She felt strangely, electrically, *alive*. The dog flattened himself in front of her and gave her the hard stare in case she planned on resuming the chase. Back at the house, Drew was wailing.

Freya caught up then and, with her hand on Ani's bent back, crouched to look in her face. "Ani? Ani, what the hell?" Then, "Babe, let's go inside."

Ani had hurt her ankle. With her arm around Freya's shoulder, she limped back down the road, Jesus instinctively bringing up the rear.

"What's going on?" Freya whispered. "Who was that?"

"I don't know. But I've seen him three times now." It had to be the same person. The same man.

Drew was crying and flapping his arms like a child of two, not eight—because they'd run off and left him and Ani had yelled. Or because the book had slid out of his lap and now lay splayed on the stairs. Ani hobbled inside to strip off her muddy clothes while Freya tended to him.

Once Drew was settled in his room, Freya came to the kitchen where Ani sat now with her foot up on a chair, holding closed her bathrobe and shivering. The shock settling on Ani had already passed through the normally Zenlike Freya. Instead, Freya's face, peppery with pale freckles, bunched. She yanked open the freezer drawer and began, furiously, to fill a zip-lock with ice.

"What three times?" she asked.

With a cowed "Thanks," Ani took the ice pack. "He was at the school the day before yesterday."

Freya's grey eyes widened, but she kept her voice low. *"What?"*

"Then I saw him yesterday on our walk. I think it was the same guy. I'm not completely sure." But she was. This time, through the rear window of the truck, Ani had glimpsed a flash of red. Red truck, red hat. A veritable red alert.

"We're calling the police," Freya announced.

"I'll get dressed." Using the table as support, Ani rose and limped out.

The question she'd been dreading came upon her return. Freya was waiting, arms in their fluttery sleeves folded across her chest. "Why didn't you tell me?"

But by then Ani had thought of a suitable reply: she hadn't

wanted to cause needless alarm. It was a lie. She'd merely wanted some space around her own feelings, which had felt so *normal*. Freya, of course, was the grand marshal of appropriate feelings. Since the truck had passed, she'd already delivered magnificently on shock and fury. Now, moved by Ani's consideration, she reached for her so that Ani felt pulled into the embrace of a loving, many-armed goddess. They only released each other when heavy footsteps sounded on the wooden steps.

Freya went to answer the knock, speaking briefly to the officer before leading him to the kitchen.

He looked in his late thirties, closely shorn, face the colour of a pink eraser. His vest bulked him up further, POLICE printed boldly across it, in case anyone missed the badges and the gun. Ani, who'd seated herself again with her foot elevated, found herself uncomfortably eye level with the gun. There were individual pouches on his belt too, for bullets, she presumed.

He listened to her account with a fixedly neutral face. "And you're sure it was the same person?"

"It was the same truck both times," Ani told him.

"And you saw the truck by the school too?"

"No."

"But it was the same man driving it? Can you describe him?"

Ani glanced at Freya, whose Zen was clearly being tested again. "I didn't get a look at his face. The hat was the same. A red ball cap."

He rubbed the shaved back of his neck.

"Look," Freya said, stepping forward. "We want you to take this seriously."

"Understood, ma'am." He addressed Ani again. "But you weren't threatened in any way? He didn't *say* anything?"

Would she have to point out the obvious? Walking on a country road while female? While queer? A truck stops. "I felt intimidated." Of course, this was after the fact. Yesterday, she'd barely registered the truck.

Freya slammed her hand on the table and both Ani and the officer startled. "We don't want to wait to be threatened!"

Down the hall, something thumped. They all turned to see Jesus in the doorway, the triangles of his ears pricked up. Freya made a shooing motion and he turned and clicked away.

Freya whispered now. "By the time there's a threat, it's often too late. We have a *child*."

It wasn't about Drew, or any of the children, Ani realized then. It couldn't be. He knew Drew would be in school, yet he'd come and found her on the road. As though punched, Ani curled in the chair.

"What is it, babe?" Freya asked.

Ani thought of something. "Can you check the truck?" she asked the officer. "Find out who he is?"

"Did you get the licence?" he asked.

"No, but how hard would it be to track down a truck like that?" She pointed to their phones on the counter and Freya brought Ani's over. *Old Chevy truck chrome bumper*, she thumbed, then flicked through the images until she found a similar one in turquoise. One last flick brought up the exact truck in a stock photo. She thrust the phone at him.

He perked up. "Looks like, maybe, a 72?"

WHO WAS HE? Ani couldn't fathom it. Neither could Freya, who got Ani to recount each sighting in detail while she made lunch.

"Jesus saw him first," Ani told her. "From *yards* away."

For his services as their saviour, Freya rewarded him with a handful of liver treats. She dropped a kiss on Ani's head.

"I wish you'd told me. You're supposed to tell me everything."

"I'm sorry," Ani said, and she was—now. Also freshly awed by her formidable wife.

"Officer," Freya mocked as she flipped the grilled cheese. "I'm wondering if I could ask you to do a little detective work?" She executed a chopping motion with the spatula. "I'll kill him if he comes near Drew."

The phone rang during lunch, but it was Freya's mother, not the officer. Ani mimed zipping her lips. When Freya nodded, Ani pressed prayer hands to her cheek.

Nap, she mouthed.

Jesus rose and followed her to the bathroom, where Ani took a couple of painkillers for her ankle, then to the bedroom where she held the covers up for him, whispering that he should get out if he heard Freya coming to bust them. With his muzzle resting on her stomach and Ani rubbing the soft inside of his ears, she fell asleep.

She dreamed that she was being watched, that it had been going on for some time. There was no obvious watcher, though, just a strong, discomfiting sensation of being stared at. Then she was standing in the room of a house she didn't know. A living room. There was a couch. She turned a circle, trying to locate the eyeless source. There, behind the door. The air around her felt weighted, like it would soon rain stones.

Her eyes flew open. Drew stood by the bed, book held like a shield across his chest. His eyes flicked to the side. A wave of relief, and love, crashed over her.

"Hi, sweetie," she said, sticky from the dream. Snippets of it clung to her unpleasantly, like a spiderweb accidentally walked through. "Did anyone phone?"

"Grandma."

Drew didn't want to get close to other people, but neither did he want to be alone. Freya must have slipped out to the workshop. Jesus, Ani realized then, was gone.

"Sit beside me while you read?" she asked Drew.

He climbed up and, leaning against the headboard, opened the book. It was a university-level genetics textbook that Ani had bought for him online, though Freya had introduced the topic, wanting to explain his complicated parentage—Ani's egg, fertilized from a catalogue, and tucked into Freya's readied body. The image Drew was studying showed a bright bar code of horizontal strips stacked six or seven high, each comprised of irregularly distributed vertical bands—red, blue, green, yellow—some lines very thin, others wider. A gaudy pattern reminiscent of 60s-era upholstery.

"That's a genome," Drew said. "Read it."

Of course it was too hard for him. Wasn't it? Ani read, "'Each nucleus contains six feet of DNA.' Amazing, isn't it?"

"It's amazing," Drew said in monotone.

She read on about the helixes and nucleotides, about A, C, G, and T. Drew kept nodding, and Ani, too, marvelled that she was somehow composed of these bright, furled ribbons. All at once she understood why this current obsession had so easily displaced Drew's preceding ones, which had included electricity, Baby Jesus and his ability to appear simultaneously in nativity scenes around town, and black holes. It would be a relief for him to see other people as colourful abstractions. This could be a picture of anyone. Her or him, side by side, not touching. The feeling in the dream came back, and how she'd woken to Drew's troubled eyes trained on her for once.

Ani looked away from the book then, as though the image might trigger a seizure.

The back screen door released its long sour note. Ani heard Freya say, "Just a sec," then the metallic slap. She sailed into the bedroom, breathless and flushed from running, dog at her heel, phone to her ear. When she saw Drew, she said, "Sweetie, take Jesus to your room."

As soon as Drew left, Freya closed the door behind him. "Okay, I'm putting you on speaker now." She tapped the phone and dropped beside Ani on the bed.

"So I had a chat with him. He drives your road a lot. He says he was never by the school."

"And you believe him?" Freya asked.

"I don't have a concrete reason not to at the moment."

"So who is he?" Ani asked.

"Ma'am, I can't tell you that."

THE MOOD IN the house changed with the phone call, or rather, after Ani said, "How concrete does the reason need to be? A chunk of it tossed through the window?"

Freya pulled her drapey sweater around herself. Speculation about the driver ceased.

They'd entered a much-argued territory. According to Freya, half the folks who lived on the Sunshine Coast now had been priced out of Vancouver, just as they, Ani and Freya, had been priced out of Toronto. Shake any tree here and a commuting professor—a *queer* commuting professor!—was sure to fall out. Among the old-timers, aging hippies like Freya's parents far outnumbered the rednecks. There was even a Rainbow Social Club that Freya kept wanting them to join.

That night, Freya slid under the covers while Ani was reading *The New Yorker*. "Is there a chance that you could be mistaken?" she asked.

Mistaken? Ani had routed the guy from the playground, even chased his truck! She stared at Freya's gently dusted profile. "Meaning?"

"You told me at first that you weren't sure he was the same person as at the school."

"I know I did. But I *am* sure."

Freya turned toward her. "If you *were* sure, why did you say you weren't?"

Ani sighed. "I didn't want to frighten you."

Freya frowned a moment longer. "Maybe he *was* just driving by. You have a habit of assuming the worst of people."

"Well," Ani said, too glibly, "people usually follow through."

"Do they?" Freya asked her. "Really? Because it feels to me like an excuse. Maybe you would enjoy life more here if you connected with other people."

The loot bag mother came to mind. The school year was three-quarters over and this was the only party Drew had been invited to. Unlike Ani, Freya would not have found a way to take umbrage at his inclusion. She would have dragged them all there so that Ani and Drew could sit awkwardly in the corner, feeling miserable.

"Another thing, Ani," Freya said. "I've been operating on the assumption that we're always absolutely honest with each other."

"Yes!" Ani said. "We are!"

"I hope so." Freya leaned in and kissed her—a peck, nothing like the kiss in the garden that morning—then turned off her light.

THE NEXT MORNING, though Ani's ankle felt fine and she yearned to walk, she couldn't face going down that road, not even in the company of Freya and Drew. Nor did she want them to walk Jesus without her. When Freya suggested this, instead of explaining her fear, Ani got prickly and proprietary until Freya's hand, firm on her shoulder, silenced her.

"He's Drew's dog, remember?"

So Ani ended up sitting alone on the back steps throwing the ball to Jesus. She understood that Freya's doubts were reasonable given her changing story, yet they still hurt. At the same time, Freya was hurt that Ani hadn't immediately told her what was going on. It was a stalemate rather than an argument. When they argued, they only had to go to bed to make things right.

Once, shortly after they'd moved here, Ani had had a go at honesty. They'd spent the day rearranging the rooms and hanging art, domestic decisions that Freya cared a lot about and Ani not at all. Ani could live in a cave.

Finally, Ani had snapped. "I'm just not good at this!"

"You're doing great!" Freya replied.

But Ani had not been talking about the rugs rolled and dragged from room to room. She had not meant the furniture.

After Jesus finally tired of the ball, she brushed his silky coat until a dark wad of fur clogged the metal teeth. She prised it out and left it on the railing.

All day, birds came and went, mocking her.

*

ON MONDAY, SHE decided to walk the other way—to town. To be on the safe side, she'd take the highway, which, after about fifteen minutes, bisected their road. She could have left Jesus off-leash until then but found herself wanting to keep him close.

This was the direction she'd chased the truck on Saturday. Why, she wondered now. She'd done it without thinking, just hurled herself after it, *like anyone would*.

The lots were more thickly treed here, or the houses, newer, had been built farther back. In either case, the only sign of habitation was a number on a post at the end of each drive. Razory bales of bramble grew in the ditches, their tiny green grenades just forming. Each time a car passed, Ani, unable to step off the road, tensed, despite every driver's cordial swerve.

Then a bicycle appeared in the distance with a large dog running abreast. A Rottweiler? Ani commanded Jesus to sit. Yawning, he settled tidily on his black haunches, tracking with his eyes the approaching bike and dog. Could he hear her pounding heart?

Dog and cyclist passed, long tongue flapping from the side of the loping Rottweiler's mouth. The cyclist lifted one set of fingers off his handlebar.

Ani exhaled. "Okay, Jesus."

They walked on and, a few minutes later, the subdivision on the outskirts of town came into view. She felt her body relax. Shortly after that, they reached the highway. From there they strode in perfect ease down the long hill with its view over the silvery, island-clotted strait.

The main street in Gibsons followed the shore with the old yellow pub guarding the entrance to the wharf. They took the concrete steps down to the beach and walked there, Jesus, unleashed now, barking as he herded the incoming tide. Under

Ani's feet, broken shells and barnacles crunched like she was stepping on shipwrecked china. Several sailboats motored past, sails furled, ropes forming empty triangles of windless air. These were, she remembered, the *Hempen Hands* in the poem.

A thought came to her then, standing on the beach watching the dog's antics. She might lose them all: Drew, Freya. Jesus too.

Ani whistled. They walked on to the set of steps that led back up to the street, where she leashed Jesus again. Judging by the sudden surge of traffic, the ferry must have just got in; a car braked for them to cross. On the other side of the street, they turned in the direction of home.

She would be alone then—a lone woman—the very state she continually orchestrated for herself, yet the thought made her dry-mouthed with panic now. To distract herself, she kept one eye on the shop windows—housewares store, tourist trap, realty office. A clothing boutique that featured Freya's designs on faceless mannequins. *Local!* With her back to the oncoming traffic, she was slow to notice a vehicle behind them, matching their pace. Then she heard it and swung around.

A flash of red, like something bursting in her eye. She was staring right at him. Grimy cap, stringy fringe of butterscotch hair, narrowed eyes. His lips were thin. He barely had lips, but the mouth opened and a word flew though the open passenger window. It was so *odd*, that word. He fired it straight into her face—to Ani, he screamed it—so that before the shock, there was, briefly, puzzlement. Jesus understood, though, and responded in kind, barking, rearing up and pawing the air, jerking so hard the leash cut into her hand. He seemed to want to rip free and pursue the truck, which had already veered into the empty oncoming lane and sped off.

The few pedestrians on the sidewalk stepped aside. One of them muttered, "Jesus Christ, lady. Get your dog under control."

OUTSIDE THE WORKSHOP, the risk-taking sewist was on her phone, back to the cab as it pulled up. Released, Jesus bounded over to greet her. Ani, meanwhile, stumbled into the house for her wallet, returned with a twenty, and waved the driver off.

In the workshop, the sewists were on break, a couple of them stretching with Freya, waiting for the kettle to boil. Ani so rarely encroached on Freya's domain that the sight of her in the doorway caused Freya's face to slide.

"Ani? What happened?"

Ani walked out and Freya followed. Not until they were inside the house and in the bedroom, Ani sinking onto the bed, did she allow herself to react. Freya held her while she sobbed, the thousand loving arms stroking her back.

He'd come after her, she told Freya, and this time, he did threaten her. And she'd seen him, clearly.

"Oh, babe," Freya said. "What did he say?"

"It was so weird what he said. Like he was . . ."

"What?"

"Trying to kill me with a word. If he'd had a gun, he would have."

"A gun? My God. What did he say?"

A knock sounded at the back door. Ani looked fearfully at Freya, who seemed to assume it would be one of the sewists. Holding up a finger, she went to answer it. Ani heard her say, "Kenzie?" The risk-taker. She heard the screen door's off-key plaint as Freya stepped outside.

Ani lay back, hands over her eyes, picturing the narrow-eyed face, memorizing it. The slight hook in the nose. Who was he? She might have conjured him out of her own assumptions about the people here. But didn't that mean that she'd been right?

Freya appeared in the bedroom doorway. "Ani? Can you come to the kitchen?"

Kenzie was sitting at their table, bent over the dog, scratching vigorously behind his ears, Jesus's tail swishing back and forth across the floor. Ani pulled him away by the collar. The girl looked up then and Ani saw her pink pierced nose and smudged cheeks. Most of her makeup had washed off, leaving her eyes nakedly beautiful.

"It's okay, Kenzie," Freya said. "Tell Ani what's going on." At the same time, she guided Ani into a chair and, taking the hand not holding Jesus's collar, wove their fingers together.

"What's going on?" Ani asked, looking from Freya to the girl.

It came out of the girl's mouth, the same word: "Bullet." Ani jerked back in her chair, but Jesus's head cocked.

"He's my brother's dog," Kenzie moaned. Her eyes overflowed.

"He's our dog!" Ani said. "We've had him for years!"

Freya squeezed her hand. "Two and a half years."

"I would have taken him!" the girl cried. "He left him with that stupid bitch."

"Who?" Ani asked.

"His so-called girlfriend. Who hauls him off to the SPCA." She sniffed, wiped snot on her sleeve. She wouldn't meet Ani's eye, but instead addressed Jesus. "I didn't know until I ran into her, like, months later. I wanted to fucking kill her!"

Ani gaped. "Are you working here because of Jesus?"

The girl looked genuinely shocked. "No! I didn't even know

he was here! I hadn't seen him for so long I almost didn't recognize him. You took good care of him. Didn't they, Bullet?"

Jesus whimpered.

"Don't call him that," Ani snapped.

"It's not because of Bu— Jesus," she told Freya, whom she would look at. She brought her hands together, begging. Chipped black polish, cheap silver rings. "I want to stay. Please let me. This is the best job I've ever had. I didn't even tell him Bullet was here, but last week? When I had the flat tire? He picked me up in the truck and saw him. Ever since, I swear it, I've been at him to keep away."

"When did your brother get out?" Freya asked.

"Get out?" Ani said. "He's been in *jail*?"

The girl slumped, inky curtain pouring over her face. "Three weeks ago. He wants his dog back. He really, really wants him."

"He can't have him, Kenzie," Freya explained in her soft, infinitely reasonable voice. "He's Drew's dog. You know Drew needs him. We can't take Jesus away from him."

"The thing is?" Kenzie lifted her face, apologetic, salt-washed. "He's on his way. Right now."

And then they heard it—the Truck coming up the Drive. Rackety Engine running, then—His Foot crunched Gravel— moving toward Them—as inexorable as the Stalking Tide crosses the China Sand.

Jesus stood—barked—

And then—I started—too—

For the Back Door. The Screen sang—a Jubilation—as she made her Late Escape—

"Jesus!" Ani called.

And He—He followed—close behind—

CHARITY

I.

MOTHER MOST FEARED. Merciless Our Lady of Mercy office assistant. She whose rust-dyed head barely showed above the counter, who would squinch her left eye when a beseeching student approached, meaning it was a given that you were bull-shitting and if you wanted charity, look behind her to the picture of the Blessed Virgin sharing wall space with the Nazi pope.

Marie, mother of Robbie.

Yet this morning something seemed to disrupt her innate skepticism. Curled up in bed with a pretend gut-ache, Robbie saw it cross her face like a benign tic. He faked another groan and Marie left for school.

He moved fast then—for him. Out of bed, the Bieb on loud, spliff lit. Shifting from fat-ass cheek to fat-ass cheek in time to "Die in Your Arms." Toke by toke, it lifted. That feeling that life was waterboarding him.

Then the stealth weapon of the car keys hit. "Ow!" He clutched the side of his head.

Marie was back—five feet, one inch of raw, maternal rage. "Get in the car." She retrieved her keys and left Robbie to hustle into his uniform.

Mere minutes later, he fell into the passenger seat, teeth scummed, cold sore weeping, hair a greasy, flat Bieb fail.

"You want to be a worthless stoner? Not on my watch. Your first class is …?"

When he didn't answer fast enough, she grabbed him by the ear. It hurt less than it would have if he hadn't already been high.

"Christian Living!"

At school, she made him wait in the office on the Bench of Shame. As well as hurried teachers, several girls pranced in to reinforce his non-existence while Robbie's stomach preached on its usual subject, Adolescent Hunger. Ten minutes after second bell, the counsellor finally arrived but refused to see Robbie again without an appointment.

"Marie," he tutted. "That would be favouritism, wouldn't it?"

"Get out," Marie said, apparently to Robbie.

By the time he squeezed into Christian Living, Father Patrick was in full drone. Lukas Slovo (king of the Bieb look) slumped in the seat ahead.

"What's going on?" Robbie asked.

"Volunteering. You can sign up for a retard camp or donate. Or you can write an essay."

"An essay?" Robbie's bowels clenched. "Donate what? Money?"

Lukas smirked. "Sperm."

"You're kidding, right?" Robbie said.

"No! They need the fresh stuff. For real."

Everyone was watching Talia Giovanni in the front row trying to make up her mind, nodding along with her manicured hand as it rose a few inches, sank, then rose again. Would Talia grace the retards with her hottie presence and in doing so, open unprecedented extracurricular access to normal guys (whoever *they* were)?

Up! A half-dozen hairy arms shot in the air too, but not Robbie's. He well knew his place in the order of peckers. A significant Our Lady of Mercy contingent considered him a retard too.

2.

WEEKS PASSED, AS per. Then one morning during PE, as everyone practised dribbling and Robbie dodged the balls hurled at him, Marie's blunt, heavily accented voice came down the PA system. "The following students please report to the nurse's room." "Robert Proulx," he heard, sourly, but correctly pronounced. *Prooo*. She'd just unwittingly saved his nuts; his big thighs were piebald crimson.

In his mortifying too-tight gym strip, hands clasped over his crotch, Robbie joined the line behind Steffie Barrow. Julie Kwan, ahead of Steffie, turned and whispered something to her. They both looked back at him and giggled. He was more than confused. If this was the line to donate (as Lukas Slovo had convinced him), what were the girls there for?

Behind the clasp—ominous stirrings.

Across the hall, visible through the office window, Marie was chatting with her colleagues as though she'd been possessed by a friendly demon that would release her just before the drive home. When she saw him, her face cinched like the drawstring bag he kept his bong in.

He returned to the question: what *was* going to happen? Specifically, what role were the girls playing in sperm donation? So compelling, it distracted him from the more obvious question: who exactly was collecting sperm from sixteen-year-old boys?

From his position at the end of the line, he could see that each donor was admitted one at a time and was, furthermore, only in the room a few minutes—surely not long enough! Lukas sauntered out next, making a beating-off gesture as he passed Robbie, who immediately found himself facing a full-on gym-short insurrection. Julie went in, then Steffie. Lukas, he noticed, had not returned to the gym but was lingering nearby with Michael Dea and Jason Mackie—"the Triad," Robbie thought of them.

Robbie's turn. He looked in at the nurse, who was old with glasses on a beaded chain.

"Name?" She riffled through her sheaf of papers. "Here you are. Robert Proolks. Have a seat."

He settled on the very cot where he'd so often lain with real gut-aches brought on by maliciously hurled balls, or spitballs, or threats upon his balls. Adding to his confusion now—a hopped-up trepidation. *What? What was going to happen?*

The nurse's back was to him as she messed about with her stuff. To calm himself, he fixed his gaze on her neutral hump. But then she turned and Robbie saw the freakishly long cotton swab in her hand.

"Where are you going to stick *that*?"

"Open," she said, unnecessarily. Horror had already loosened his jaw.

And the door flew open too, on the Triad still in the hallway, accompanied now by a gaggle of girls. Writhing, thrusting, panting—an orgiastic flash mob. "You go, Robbie! *Huh-huh-huh! Huh-huh-huh!*"

Scowling, the nurse reached over and slammed the door.

"Idiots." She motioned for him to open again. One cheek, then the other, scrubbed with the swab.

But she must have seen it in his eyes—how it felt to live every morning and afternoon as the joke's butt end. Because, when she was done, she gave his shoulder a consoling pat.

"Thank you. You did good."

3.

THE FOLLOWING YEAR, the pope resigned. With the office staff in the lunchroom, Lukas Slovo, Michael Dea, and Robbie Proulx (goaded into the prank) infiltrated the unlocked premises and took selfies of themselves Nazi-saluting His former Holiness. Marie was around the corner by the photocopiers collating handouts. She did not hesitate to turn them in.

"Your *mom's* a Nazi," Lukas muttered while they all waited on the Bench of Shame.

For Robbie, the suspension felt more like a reprieve. He barely had to smoke! And since he was already flunking everything except Christian Living, which only required Christian vital signs to pass, when the two weeks were over, he announced to Marie that he wasn't going back.

"You'll really turn out to be a nobody now. Probably a criminal too."

Back in Montreal, her father had gone to jail for swindling the wrong people. Marie had built a world view around the event, which was that people were good or evil, mainly the latter.

Robbie made a joke about her seeing him on TV one day, on one of those true crime shows that she watched.

"You think that's funny? If you knew anything about it, you'd shut your mouth. Another thing, I'm not running a charity. You can pay rent like anywhere."

She added, "No drugs."

4.

THE STEAM THAT rose from the steely tub opened wide the pores. The drip-drip-drip of sweat, and the never-healed cold sore. The drain trap filled with crud, the green bin alley-lugged. The rash that bubbled under industrial gloves.

Dishwasher loaded—plates, utensils, flatware. Serving stations stocked, counters bleached, glasses dropped.

The shards swept up.

The empty promise: *Come for a job, stay for a career!* The excuse: "As the face of the restaurant, the server is always happy and smiling. Does that sound like you, Robert? How about sticking with dishwashing a little longer?"

And seeing that it was a soft October 2:00 a.m. as he left the SkyTrain station, he decided not to bus, but walked the rest of the way under the cold, clear dome of stars, getting high as he listened to how Drake had started from the bottom too.

5.

NINE MONTHS PASSED, as per, and Robbie started at the bottom again. Shipments received, schlepped, shelved. Warehouse swept. Bathrooms too, including the Ladies, all under the direction of Angelo. A head shorter, goateed, Angelo was teaching Robbie to drive the forklift.

"Easier if you already know how to drive a car. Why can't you drive a car?"

"Because if I scratched it or anything, my mom would kill me," Robbie told him.

"She just says that. She loves you more than anything."

Angelo's mother probably loved him more than anything. All the women at Tri-City Liquidators (three) couldn't keep their hands off him, yet from Robbie they recoiled, despite his gallant unjamming of the tampon dispenser.

Standing by, hands on hips, Angelo talked Robbie through a jerky reverse. Shift to neutral, parking brake applied, tines raised.

"You are doing it, my man!"

Encouragement had the opposite effect on Robbie, who was practiced at reading sarcasm in even the most earnest praise. It didn't help that Angelo wouldn't let him smoke before getting behind the wheel. The tines struck the box. It tumbled off the shelf, splitting open as it hit concrete and spraying glacier-scented Speed Sticks like a gangster's bullets. Angelo danced to avoid them.

While Robbie was bent over gathering the strewn deodorant, he felt one slip into his back pocket.

"And you should shower more," Angelo said. "Like, every day. Then maybe, who knows? We might swipe some babes together, eh?"

That night at dinner, Robbie asked Marie, "Why did you never tell me to shower?"

Her fork fell from her hand. "I bathed you every day of your life until you could do it on your own! I taught you to clean under your foreskin! I'd never even seen one before I saw yours!"

"Okay, okay."

"Do you think my mother told me to take a bath? She didn't because—"

"Because she was dead. I know. And then your dad went to jail."

"Are you cleaning under your foreskin? No, don't tell me! I don't care! You pulled your hand out of mine and said you didn't want to hold it anymore. You were a big boy. This without thanking me for anything. If you want to stew in your own juices, go ahead. Your rent is due."

He didn't know what she was talking about half the time.

6.

Robbie, 18
First...
Word: mama (Yeah, I'm a mama's boy.)
Job: altar boy
Music download: "Love Lockdown"
Kiss: Talia Giovanni (Okay, it was a dream.)

"MAMA?" ROBBIE SAID. He had himself supplied Talia's name.

Angelo, Tinder author, said, "Ladies love that. Says you're respectful. That's a bop song, too."

Robbie's profile picture, also by Angelo, showed him in a slimming black tee leaning against the forklift, arms crossed to hide his tits. They argued about the other photos, of which Angelo insisted there be a minimum of four to reflect his personality.

"I don't have a personality, Angelo."

"Angelo, 26" posed shirtless on the forklift, shirtless at the beach, shirtless in the bathroom mirror, as well as in an ivory barong tagalog embroidered with flowers. Angelo may have been small, but his pipes were XXL. He was probably right-swiped so hard the force of it knocked him off his feet.

7.

SHOWER, SMEAR THE glacier scent into his pits. Shave around the goatee and the 'stache that hid the scar next to his lip. Prepare to meet the faces that he'd seen. The four that actually swiped right.

The nerve-jangling wait despite the spliff. His fatness through the window glimpsed. The swipes that changed to left.

The hands that Rolled Up the rim and lost, that declined with a tiny wave the eager offer of a Timbit. The question, "Am I what you expected?"

Robbie's reply (his hand upon his chest). "You're better!"

Because he knew better than to expect anything.

8.

"YOU'RE BETTER!" ROBBIE said, and "Marian, 22, Jewish" blushed a deeper shade of red. Especially shy about her breasts, she kept X-ing them with her forearms. They were the hottest thing about her! Tied for second, the rounded bonus of hips and thighs, the sproingy hair. Even her eyes were outsized, like anime. She was studying psychology to help with her own "messed-upedness" (revealed on her profile; they did not discuss it).

Marian accepted a Timbit and for the rest of the hour wore a sugar flake on her nose. Afterward, when he visited the can, he saw his goatee similarly flaked!

On the SkyTrain, he thumbed, *did you here about that couple that got married at Timmys?* But didn't send.

Marie was watching the news in her bathrobe when he got home, pale eyes narrowed against the world's bullshit. "Well? Did she show?"

Only then did it register: the similarity of their names.

9.

SPIDER-MAN 2, THEN the walk to English Bay. The bench on which they sat, the hands they held. The moon, a silver skid mark on the water, a sheen on sand. Their fourth date. Time to kiss her!

He didn't dare.

After a long silence, Marian asked, "You don't find me attractive, do you?"

"What? No! I mean, yes!"

She lunged for him. So soft, her mouth! Opening, it opened his. When they finally came up for air, she said, "My place?"

In the near-empty bus, she asked him to tell her something embarrassing about himself.

"Embarrassing?"

How to begin? Spit it out like the spliff's butt end? The mottled thighs, the jeers, the Prooz/Poo-Z/Prooks of his former days? Then he remembered the debacle of grade eleven. How, late for class, he signed up to be a donor.

"Of what?" Marian asked.

"That's the thing. This buddy of mine said sperm." Robbie clapped his big hand against his big forehead. "Stupid, I know!"

He told her, too, about the girls in line. "I actually thought... I mean, *cringe*. I thought they might be there to *help* the boys. But when my turn came, the nurse took out this honking Q-tip. Where the hell was she going to stick it?"

Seeing the look Marian's face, he hastened to add, "She stuck it in my mouth."

"So what were you donating?"

"It was to check our blood type or something. I don't know. Nothing ever happened."

Sensing her disappointment, he wondered if he should go on and tell her about the snickering mob who'd set him up. How, for the rest of his time at OLOM, everyone greeted him with the jerk-off gesture.

"What about you?" he asked instead.

Marian turned away. Their eyes met in the bus window, superimposed on the half-lit buildings blurring past.

"It's okay," he told her. "You don't have to tell me anything."

"No, I *have* to. I have"—she X-ed her chest—"three nipples."

Where? Robbie wanted to ask before he realized what the confession implied. Would he shortly . . . he, Robbie . . . know the answer?

Now he dared—to push aside the mass of sproings and find her lips. Necking, they overshot her stop.

Marian lived close to the university. Side gate, deck, and planter, the hidden key that she extracted. Ushered inside, he saw a white-tiled kitchen, all granite and stainless steel, dimly lit by lights above the sink. From the silence of the house, he guessed her parents were out, or in bed.

Steps away, down a short hall, Marian's room. She pulled him in, leaving the door ajar.

In the deeper darkness, clothing rustled, but he saw nothing, not even when she stood before him, positioning his hands. (So soft, her breasts!) She demonstrated how she wanted to be squeezed and, while Robbie complied, she worked at his jeans. One yank and he was stripped to the knees.

He sank onto the bed. By then his eyes had adjusted enough to see her glowing thighs and booty jiggling over to the dresser, then her glowing breasts—pale and ample, and (seemingly) singly nippled—jiggling back. The square of Cellophane pressed into his palm.

"You put it on," he said, in case he blew it.

Pushed backward, trussed below the knees, he lay there—a throb awaiting sheathing.

The white teeth that tore the square, the latex coolness, then. The slithering squeeze, the warming glide. A mysterious odour filled the room, a yeasty tang with fainter notes of spermicide and melting butter. Robbie exploded with a shout, then Marian did.

Afterward, bawling loudly into the pillow, Marian's perfumed arms gathered him up. Robbie had *become* his dick, pulsing with love and gratitude even as he limpened. When he opened his eyes, he saw Marian's face in the stronger light still flushed from her exertions. The buttery smell was stronger, too. From down the hall, humming, clattering.

"I have to go," Robbie said in a panic. "I'm working in the morning."

Marian eased the condom off, knotted and solemnly handed it to him while he pulled up his jeans. She wrapped herself in a kimono. Hand in hand, they walked to the kitchen.

"Oh, hi Daddy. This is Robbie."

Behind the island stood a man with glasses and greying curls. He smiled at Marian then, switching the spatula to his left hand, extended the right to Robbie across the stove.

"Nice to meet you, Robbie. You two must be hungry. Grilled cheese?"

In Robbie's front pocket, his souvenir oozed its virgin contents down his thigh. "Thanks, but I've got to get going."

"I'll have one," Marian said. "Is Mommy up?"

"Gone to bed."

"You'll meet her next time," Marian told Robbie as she led him to the door and, in full view of her father, filled his mouth with tongue.

*

10.

AND THE AFTERNOON and the evening of every weekend—spent together, screwing. Like creatures driven solely by the need to couple, they squeezed, balled, rejoiced—despite the frequent presence of her parents, which Robbie could not get used to. He was pretty sure that if Marie caught them at it, she would set fire to them both.

Smoothed by her long fingers (his hair, his dick), spent... asleep...They stretched out on the bed, Robbie and Marian, singing, "Love Never Felt So Good," a song he learned to love, because Marian did.

Yet he had a question. *Can I see it?*

After rising to use the can and probably running into her mother, who would ask, "Do you two lovebirds want a snack?" (was she for real?), he wondered: should he return and pose the nipple question? For no matter their coital position, Marian managed to keep the mystery of it tucked under her right arm. After four months, an alluringly pink edge of aureole was all he'd glimpsed.

11.

"BUT NO ONE can see it. Why does it bother you so much?"

"It's not about other people. I hate it. Why do you keep bringing it up?"

12.

MARIE AIMED THE meat probe. She'd dressed as though for Mass, in nylons, heels, and a high-necked blouse, but with makeup too. What could it mean?

Hovering behind her, Robbie gaped into the oven. "Mom? Is that a ham? She's Jewish!"

"That's the first I've heard of it," Marie lied.

When she withdrew the probe and saw him still there, diarrheal with apprehension, she snapped, "I said go to the bathroom and light a match! I can smell your stink from here!"

He went and got his lighter. "What's that for?" she demanded. "You're not taking drugs still, are you?"

"I'm not 'taking drugs.'"

The doorbell rang and Robbie practically raced Marie to get there first, opening the door on a harried Marian tightly compressed into jeans, bearing a bottle of wine that Marie would not drink.

"God, it took forever to drive here!"

All the way to suburban Coquitlam, the grounds where he'd been stomped, the lands where, until Marian, he'd strived for a state of perpetual wastedness. For seven months he'd postponed this invitation.

"You eat ham, don't you?" he asked her now.

Marie shoved him aside, baring her teeth in welcome. Robbie remembered how, at school, he used to wonder if an imposter had taken his mother's place. Here she was again, the false Marie, smiling with a mouth lipsticked a dried-blood shade that matched her hair.

She turned to Robbie. "Do that thing I just told you to do. She'll want to wash her hands before we eat."

He hurried off to the can with the lighter, hoping the air would ignite and immolate him.

Back in the kitchen, the ham bulged over the platter's rim and Marian, apparently unfazed, was chattering away. Her university courses, her parents. Her mother was a child psychologist, her father a professor of biomechanics researching the motion of flagellum.

"The motion of what?" Marie asked, the corner of her phony smile twitching. Here was one of her many contradictions. Education was everything, but God help you if you showed it off.

"Flagellum."

"Macaroni salad?" asked the false Marie. To Robbie: "Sit."

Now Marian began questioning Marie, causing Robbie's bowels to loosen again. "You're from Montreal? I love that city! Have you been, Robbie?"

He shook his head with vigour enough to expel a scorpion from his ear canal.

"You have," Marie said. "You were born there."

He was? "Excuse me for a sec."

In the can, he sat with head in hands, listening to Marian's questions over the fan's ruckus. Would his criminal bloodline be revealed? Marian would want details, details that, as a child, Robbie had been discouraged from learning. "What you don't know won't hurt you," drove the plot of fairy tales, but in Robbie's case, accompanied as it was by Marie's infamous ear-twist, had stamped out all curiosity.

He flushed, washed his hands. When he shut off the tap and could hear them again, he had to wonder if his oft-grabbed ears were working right. Were Marie and Marian *speaking French*? He had literally *never* heard it from Marie.

"You speak French?" he asked Marian when he returned.

"She doesn't," Marie said, and though this barely counted as an insult from Marie, Marian took offence. Her dark eyes, swivelling to meet Robbie's, brimmed with WTF.

But then they switched to English, and safer topics. Robbie's fork lifted mouth-ward, inserting food he dryly swallowed. He decided that if Marian left him after this, he would set himself on fire.

Finally, Marie ordered him to clean up. While the two women headed for the living room, he hurried through the chore, taking a half-empty garbage bag to the garage where he could self-medicate before rejoining them.

They were side by side on the sofa by then, paging through a photo album. He took a seat next to Marian. There he was—a blob in the bathtub joyously slapping the water. The hand that had, presumably, just cleaned under his foreskin held him upright while the other crookedly aimed the camera.

"So cute!" Marian kissed his cheek.

What he saw on the next page rocked his world: Marie, no older than a teenager, gazing down as she cradled him. He'd always thought of his mother as old because she dressed and acted like the other office assistants. Once, in a defaced social studies textbook, he'd read their scrawled names under a picture of Easter Island statues. *Mrs Lowrie, Mrs Vassari, Miss Proulx* ... In this photograph his baby face, turned from the camera, was lost in Marie's unbuttoned blouse. (What hand took *that* picture?)

"Mom?" he asked. "Was I *breastfed*?"

An arm shot out from the other side of Marian and thumped him hard.

13.

AS EXPECTED, AFTER the visit, Marian had questions, questions he was supposed to answer without making himself sound even more like a clown. Bozo from the Burbs! The facts Robbie had scraped together over time were scant and always seemed made up, or at least strongly influenced by *Unusual Suspects* and *48 Hours*. The swindler father (grandfather to him), the "wrong" people that he'd crossed (who?).

Marie and her older sister (never named), already motherless, having to fend for themselves.

So, one evening, he asked Marie, "Why don't you talk to your sister?"

She was making herself a cup of tea. Her hand froze, bag mid-air, dripping. A contraction of rage passed through her tiny body. "Who?"

"You told me after your dad went to jail, you and your sis—"

She cut him off. "What you don't know—"

"Yeah, yeah," Robbie said, walking out. He didn't actually want to know.

More worrisome were Marian's questions about him. "Don't you have *any* ambition? Why not get a better job?"

"I just got a raise," Robbie told her. "And all my friends work at Tri-City."

Angelo, Doris the inventory manager, and Kimmy and Andrea in Accounting, who petted and flirted with him, and who'd organized his Safeway birthday cake, *You are doing it, my man!* icing-writ. (Even a little plastic forklift!)

"Why don't you ask *her* about your father?" Marian said. Meaning, Marie, a.k.a. the rudest person Marian had ever met.

The lower clench. "She doesn't talk about him."

"That implies one thing: trauma. Get it out in the open. Process it. You two need therapy. She's sooo angry. What if she was raped?"

"What would I do with that information, honey? I mean, how would it help to find out that my father was a rapist? Anyway, I don't have a father. All he is to me is sperm."

Marian rose from her bed and, lifting her kimono off the hook, slid her bare white arms into the sleeves. "I think you should ask her. Don't you know how stuck you are, Robbie?"

14.

THE WAY HER arm, white and bare, lay along the pillow, petal almost visible. If she would just, if he could just.

The prurient urge that stretched out his neck. The goatee that brushed her nose. The sleeping hand that rubbed its knuckles against the tickle, then flopped back down. But not before Robbie shifted his head upon the pillow.

His face was nearly in her pit now, nostrils filling with perfume and sweat, and right there, inches from his eyes—the forbidden nipple. Strangely, it didn't match the other two, but was half their size, its center hidden. If he could touch it with his tongue, the way he'd knelt before her and licked into the corners of her afternoons, lingering until she fell groaning upon her back. If he could place his lips around this unloved part of her and love it, its center would surely rise from its modest fold and overflow. *Then* she would know his love. *Really* know it.

He dared!

Marian sat up in bed and, making the X, screamed.

15.

STOP TEXTING ME I don't want to see you anymore

16.

"FORGET ABOUT HER. She's a princess. Her father, Professor of Flatulence. Big deal. They think they're so smart. She didn't even wash her hands before she ate."

But he could not forget, and when Kimmy entered the Ladies and found him sobbing there, she rushed to find Angelo. Emptying the feminine hygiene receptacle had triggered Robbie. When Marian was on the rag, he would trundle back and forth to the can, tending to her.

Angelo appeared now in the doorway. "Come with me, my man."

They sat together on a crate, Angelo's bulging pipe around Robbie's despairing shoulder, his phone in hand. "Let's swipe. Come on. Look at her! She's waiting for you! We'll put your profile back up."

"I can't. I can't."

17.

THE SHIFT TO neutral, the tines raised. The soundless backward roll that Robbie himself did not perceive, lost as he was in hellish torments of regret.

The human shout inciting panic. The gear engaged and gas applied.

The human scream.

18.

THE SUBURBAN COIL, its streetlights few and far between. Their yellow, rain-washed glow.

The reek of spliff. He rubbed his eyes.

"Look, my man," Angelo said on the phone. "Accidents happen. I know you're sorry. You've told me about a hundred times. I forgive you, but I'm in a lot of pain here and need to rest. If Tri-City won't write you a reference, I will. Please. You got to stop calling me."

Looking for another job he texted Marian, who must have blocked him. In the meantime, he maintained a functioning high, tended to his cold sore, and walked around.

The streets he followed in a daze, leading him away, away, yet ever back. Where else could he go?

"You think you'll get another job looking like a Hells Angel?"

Marie told him. "You'll never get another girl either. Not the way you talk to them. No please or thank you."

"The way I talk to them? Mom? You're the only girl I've talked to in, like, six months."

"I hear you on the phone, bossing that girl around."

"Who?!"

"Don't use that tone with me!"

"Never mind. I'm going for a walk." He grabbed his stash, earbuds, coat. So his phone wouldn't get wet, he slogged all the way to the bus shelter before unpocketing it.

"Siri, play 'Love Never Felt So Good.'"

19.

EVENTUALLY HE ERRED. Staggered into the kitchen, unlit spliff glued to his lip with the cold sore's hardened seepage. Like that morning when he cranked the Bieb—grade eleven, 2.5 years before.

In walked Marie, dressed for Mass.

"What day is it?" he asked.

She tore the spliff off his face, ripping open the sore. "What's this? I said no drugs."

"It's just weed, Mom. It's practically legal."

"Not in this house." She clicked past him in church heels. "You'd better be gone when I get home. You can come back when you're clean."

"Clean? Mom? It's not heroin. It's *weed*."

The door slammed. It always did. (She was sooo angry!) Robbie went to rinse the blood out of his mouth.

Sometime later, his phone rang. Marie asked, "Where are you?"

"Bed," Robbie told her.

"Have you packed? I'm getting in the car now."

He heard her fiery exhalations, felt their singe. The pale left eye descended and, hovering before him, squinched.

"You know what?" he said. "I *am* leaving because my life is nothing but a pile of shit. THANKS TO YOU!"

20.

THREE NIGHTS AT the Days Inn and he had a plan. He'd looked up the Proulxs, who numbered 648. His luck being what it was, he'd started from the bottom. "Are you possibly related to Marie Proulx from Montreal who lives now in Coquitlam, BC?"

On the eighth call, bingo! The woman who answered, initial *Y*, coughed for what seemed a full minute, before saying, "Who wants to know?"

"Me. I'm her son, Robbie. Are you her sister?"

"What if I am?"

"I'm trying to connect to family."

The fact that she hung up didn't discourage him. He had an aunt! A *tante*, Google Translate told him, and by extension, maybe, an *oncle*, too, and *cousins* that Marie had kept from him. They didn't want anything to do with her? Neither did he!

He texted Marian. *Going to Montreal I'll send pics!* And in his mind he saw a backyard barbecue, complete with a keg (notwithstanding that it was October). All those arms open in familial welcome!

To save his dwindling funds, he slept on the bus, lulled by the thrum of wheels and the murmuring from other seats. Sometimes a louder voice would tear him from a restless dream, like en route to Calgary when an argument farther up the aisle ended with, "Shut up or I'll slit your throat."

He woke in cities where dawn glinted on mirrored walls,

in towns with names spelled out on water towers. Woke to glaciered mountains and stubbled hills. To a hundred paper cranes lifting off a flat brown field.

He slept in stations, propped against machines that whir-ringly dispensed his meals. In Regina, the glass reflected back a sasquatch trying to decide between a granola bar and a Mr. Big. He recalled the throat-slitter's growl. The other passen-gers probably thought it came from him.

Duffle lockered, he went out in search of a barber.

Babies cried, lovers whispered. Across the aisle, beneath a jacket, a hand job was administered. Sault Ste. Marie, Toronto, Kingston. The blurred sign he texted to Marian—*Montréal 138 km.* His message: *Almost there!*

And then he was, in the city of his birth, where the trees had dressed themselves in red and gold. He stepped out of the station and, plugging one ear against four honking lanes, called his aunt. "I'm here!"

She goose-honked back. *"Quoi?"*

"Robbie, Marie's son? I called before. I'm in Montreal."

21.

FROM HONORÉ-BEAUGRAND STATION, he walked ten minutes to a falafel joint. Though there was time (he was early), he feared the slop of sauce and only bought a coffee, which he gingerly transported to one of the window stools. He blew and sipped, sipped and blew, nervously studying each passerby. He might have been waiting for a date.

Then, at the precise time of their rendezvous, just as he swallowed the coffee's dregs, someone spoke.

"Well? It must be you."

Robbie turned to look at the biker lady at the next counter, the one nursing a Dr Pepper. Leather-clad—vest, boots, face—long hair bleached the colour of fluorescent lighting. Impossible to tell her age in relation to his mother, yet the same pale eyes fixed him from under heavy turquoise lids, crow-stamped at the corners. Her accent was even blunter than Marie's. In fact, she growled.

She lifted the helmet from the stool next to her and set it on the counter. Her hand, brass-knuckled with rings, patted the place. He shuffled over with his awkward bag, sat.

"What do you want from us?" she asked.

Us? Who? What *did* he want? And how should he begin? He told her he was there to visit, maybe to stay, to live. (He didn't mention how he'd hoped it would be with her.) Start again. His life had ... What? And why, why, why? Why was it so hard to say what he meant?

She interrupted. "She sent you. What does she want?"

And now he saw the squinch. On Marie's sister, it was infinitely more sinister. (I'll slit your throat.) "My mom? Nothing. She doesn't even know I'm here."

A derisive snort, a crab-handed jab.

"Whatever she told you, she's a lying little slut. She wants money? If it was so terrible, why did she have you? And *now* she sends you? After all this time? That's *extorsion*." She said the word in French. "I don't think so."

Robbie focused on staying on the stool.

"So just fuck off," she concluded, "or you might get your legs broke, eh?"

22.

THE LEAF-STREWN SIDEWALKS, the squat buildings made of brick. The blue bikes bearing down on him. Into deeper streets he went, where every sign was French—DÉPANNEUR, COUCHE-TARD, TABAGIE. Strangely, "lying" had shocked him more than "slut." Marie's biggest fault, he thought now, might have been her honesty.

The day died early here. Cold, sore-shouldered, he dropped the duffle and dug out his phone. His data had dried up in Winnipeg. On he walked, in search of free Wi-Fi.

A signal, at last detected. "Siri? Would you please tell me where the fuck I am?"

Then he saw it, right across the street, the dunce-capped roof, the boxy manse. He was Catholic! He knocked. English was understood, a call made. He was in luck. One bed left.

The man with deranged eyes who stared from the next bunk. Robbie slept clothed, wallet stuffed in stale Jockeys, phone (dead for now) clutched to his heart. Come morning, the panicked search through his bag, everything tossed out, thrown back.

The sock-footed hobble to the front desk. "What am I supposed to do without shoes?"

The sickening realization that, somewhere along the way, or during the storm-tossed night, his wallet had dislodged.

Yet he did not call home. What would he say? That they gave him a Metro pass, a coat, and too-tight shoes? That all day he rode, getting off now and then to limp around? That, stumbling upon Old Montreal at dusk, he'd sat on a curb to watch a boxing match through the window of a bar, and thought of her? The girl in the photograph (whose hand took the picture?), younger than him when she took this trip in reverse.

That he had climbed the mountain, and gone down to the river? That he couldn't sleep without his bedtime toke? Projected on the shelter walls, the netted pattern of his own withdrawing nerves. The chills and sweats. The relief offered in a universal gesture from men, hoodied and hollow-eyed, lurking in the yard. *(Fumée, fumée?)* Whatever they were smoking, it wasn't weed.

In the dying fall, he shivered on a bench beside the river. The white-haired waves stretched out their arms to him. *Come! Come!* Why should he resist? The cold would numb his throbbing head, their open mouths would open his. Brackish tongues would fill him, and then... Then he'd be the nobody he'd always been, and no shit would be given because of it.

His phone rang. He looked at it. Marie, calling to state the obvious.

"You're in trouble."

"Mom?" he begged, only to be answered, as ever, with rebuke.

"They've been calling here every day," she said. "I'm sick of answering for you."

"Who?"

"The hospital. It's about your test. I guess you have a sexually transmitted disease."

He clutched his head. "Mom? Where would I get a sexually transmitted disease?"

"I don't know and I don't care. I gave them your number. Also? You might have told me where you are. I think I deserve that."

Robbie's eyes filled then, with wind, with tears. Marie hung up.

Almost immediately, the phone rang again. A woman said his name, correctly. "Mr. Proulx?" She had such good news. "You're a match!"

"What is this?" Robbie asked.

"You volunteered. You gave a swab. In..." He heard clicking keys. "In 2012. So, a while ago."

"I'm not there anymore. I'm in Montreal."

"No problem. We can do it anywhere."

"I want to go home," Robbie said.

"Of course. Better to be close to family, though I assure you we'll make you as comfortable as possible. And we cover all expenses, Mr Proulx. You won't be out of pocket. Just think. A life will be saved."

23.

THE HOTEL, THE domed meals delivered on a tray. The successful physical.

The plane ride (his first!).

The procedure once again explained. His pelvis punctured in eight places, the marrow sucked. Dr Lalli told him, "She only had three matches. One declined outright. The other changed his mind last minute. Imagine how devastating that would be? But you? You stepped up!"

Gowns and caps, their smiles masked. He was afraid. Then midnight came.

And when he woke: the praise! "Robbie! You're the man!" "How's the pain?" "You are, quite literally, one in a million." "Two million."

Dr Lalli said, "This guy, hey?"

"I know," said the grinning nurse. He blew Robbie a kiss.

"I need my phone."

"It's right here, Robbie…Certainly, I can call her for you."

When next he woke, Marie was at his side, sobbing. "So thin! Your arms and legs! What have they done to you?"

24.

"HERE'S A VOICE from the past."

Robbie unfortunately knew it. He of the perfect Biebness. "Lukas?"

"My mom met yours at church. Said you were in the hospital."

"Out now," Robbie said. "I appreciate you calling."

"Yeah. My mom made me. She's standing right here. So, you okay?"

"Yeah. It was just two days. Long story."

The acoustics shifted as Lukas walked out of whatever room he was in. He dropped the volume on the whine. "You're not still living with your mother, are you? She used to scare the shit out of us, remember? Even now, when I hear on the news about some dismembered body found in a suitcase, I always think, 'Wow! Robbie finally did it.'"

Robbie was going to let the comment slide, but then he didn't. "You don't know shit about my mom, Lukas."

Lukas paused before conceding. "Fair enough. Hey, did you hear about Talia Giovanni? She OD'd."

"What?"

"Yeah. Last year. Terrible. Well, take care, man."

25.

IN THE WEEKS that followed, he interrupted his copious napping to hobble from bed to can, his pelvis emitting from its hollowness a Category 5 ache. Mostly he was tired, though whether this was due to the procedure, or the way he'd messed up his life, he couldn't say.

Marie, who'd stayed home from work for the first time in his life, tended to him. She didn't ask where he'd been. And if she saw upon his waking face a hint of what he knew, she quickly turned away. There'd been other times (he remembered now), especially in childhood, when she'd looked down at him in his bed like this, with something like tenderness. In the hospital, she'd sobbed as though her world was ending.

"It must have been hard," he told her one morning.

"What?"

"Coming out here all alone."

She adjusted the pillow by his head, chopping at it. "I couldn't get away fast enough."

"With a baby and everything?"

"That's why I did it!"

He thought of the bathtub picture. "Someone must have helped you."

"The sisters did."

Then the eye squinched and she stalked out, muttering until the vacuum drowned her.

26.

April 11, 2017

Dear Mr Robert Proulx,

You don't know us but we are two girls living in Tennessee, United States of America. I am Katy and I am eight and my sister Sasha is five. We were not alowd to write you for one year but now we are and so we want to say thank you for saving our momma. She is a lot better now. Our daddy thanks you too.

Yours truely,
Katy, Sasha, and Colin Montgomery

The postscript was in an adult's hand. *Ps. No words ... Will find them one day. Ann*

Daisies with smiley faces on a folded page.

27.

CHRISTMAS CAME, AS per. He received another card.

28.

THE FOLLOWING SPRING, Ann wrote. They were visiting the Oregon coast that summer and would love to pop up to Vancouver.

But I understand your need for privacy, if you'd rather not. Mostly I want you to know that I'm in complete remission. Also, that every morning when I wake up, the first thing I do is think of you.

Yet he did not reply. What would he say? That he was working as a security guard? Lots of time for tunes! Time to study too. He was finishing Adult Basic Ed, where he'd met a girl, Priti, who was. Early days! There would be time to mess up yet! Less dope now. He bought it in the government store, so what could Marie say? Nothing, if he smoked in the garage.

His bowels, in fact, churned when he thought of Ann Montgomery from Memphis, Tennessee (whom he'd googled), sitting across a restaurant table from him. He would stammer; no doubt spill. "You're not what I expected," she would have to say as, cold sore erupting, he yammered like an idiot. He couldn't disappoint her, not when he'd been given this gift. Some part of Robert Proulx lived in her, lived in that white house with the columns (Google Street View), with two cute kids (like buttons!), and a square-jawed husband who was a CPA (est. income 100+ grand a year!). It warmed him—to the bone.

OBSCURE OBJECTS

HOT IN SUMMER, cold in winter—as though weather actually reached us in the staff room. Not so: the room was *unfenestrated*. What blew over us were the perversely inverted whims of the AC system. Each teacher was assigned a carrel which felt so much like a stall that after I finally quit, I blamed it, the carrel, for the near-bovine sense of complacency that kept me working there an entire year. In the facing one, *tête-à-tête* to me, though I couldn't see her when we were both seated, was a woman I'd known in university, Janine. Janine with the unmistakable hair. Even her eyebrows and lashes and the fuzz on her arms glistened bronze. Yet she recognized me first. The day I was hired, she stood up in her carrel and, from her higher vantage, looked down into mine.

"Charlotte?" she said. "So this is it? The *inexorable* end to a degree in creative writing?"

A caramel-haired head popped up over the partition to my left. Renata, who gave me this story. Long nose, a bump on its bridge, eyebrows darker than her hair, vaguely Euro, though her big hair and laugh screamed suburban mom. Later I met Sterling, who was serving time behind the right partition, ball-and-chained there by *Practical English Usage*. He was the one who first described the room as unfenestrated. A half-dozen or so other colleagues also toiled there, thanklessly.

In the same small room stood a metal supply cupboard with a lock, the combination a countdown: 10-9-8. Every time we took a pencil or a stick of chalk, we had to update the inventory posted inside the door, initialling it so management could keep track of who was using what. The photocopy machine churned away in the corner, a beige Satanic mill. There were no class texts. We photocopied entire chapters, which made competition for the machine especially cutthroat the fifteen minutes before class. In fact, we might have developed rapport as a staff despite the isolating carrels if not for the way the machine pitted us one against the other, and the continuous noise of it, its insatiable demand for toner which no one wanted the grubby job of adding, its serial jams, the blinking green light on the map on the inside panel, which supposedly indicated the precise location of the jam, usually so deep within the hot gears and plates that no fingers dared go there; if not for the obvious disgust of the briefcased repairman who appeared every few weeks to minister to the overworked machine. We could tell he thought it was a shitty place to work and so were further divided by our shame, just as management wanted it. They were terrified we would unionize.

A private ESL college, it recruited students from all over Asia—Taiwanese boys avoiding compulsory military service, kids from Hong Kong sent over alone or with a dotty grand-parent to occupy the mansions their parents had built in Vancouver in anticipation of the upcoming Chinese handover, and Japanese kids who were, as the expression went, "nails that could not be pounded down."

Or it was a tutoring agency that catered to children of wealthy immigrants and ADHD-afflicted offspring of the Canadian-born rich. I haven't decided yet.

Janine and I had not been friends in university. I remembered her because of her hair. Now that I was sitting and she standing and leaning over my carrel wall, I could see inside her nostrils, also bronzed with tiny hairs.

"Are you still writing?" she asked.

I said I was.

"We should exchange stories sometime," Janine said.

"You're a writer?" Renata asked over the left partition.

I SENSE MORE narrative potential in the private college, so I'll use that.

The first day, I ate lunch with Renata, whose teaching schedule overlapped with mine that term. Thankfully, I didn't have the same lunch break as Janine. I didn't want to reminisce about the fiction workshop we'd taken together, or exchange news about the other students. I especially didn't want her to ask about X, whom I'd met in the workshop and had been in a two-year relationship with.

The school took up a floor of an office tower above a chi-chi new downtown mall. In the elevator on the way down to the food court Renata gathered all her caramel into a ponytail and let it go again with a sigh.

"God, I hate those cubicles," she said.

I nodded. "They make me feel like a cow."

"Or an operator in a call centre. A phone-sex call centre!"

Renata named the owner of the school, the principal, and the vice-principal, Mrs Armstrong, the only one I'd met so far. "They're our pimps. And they dupe these kids into thinking they've enrolled in some prestigious institution. Some of the staff don't even have a teaching certificate. Do you have a teaching certificate?"

I did.

"What the hell are you doing here if you have a certificate?"

"I was travelling. I just got back. I needed a job right this second."

In the food court, our students filled the tables, chopsticking shimmery chow mein from China Kitchen and imitation crabmeat California rolls from Nippon Express. "Welcome to our prestigious cafeteria," Renata said.

She told me about herself as we ate. She was married with two sons, Evan and Andrew, in grade three and four. Her primary faults—big appetite, big mouth, the heartbreak of excess abdominal fat—came from being half Italian.

"I thought Italians were dark-haired," I said.

"Southern Italians are dark. They're the dirt on the sole of the boot. Northern Italians are fair. So where were you traveling?"

"Ireland. I was at an artist colony."

"So you're a real writer, unlike Janine who just goes around telling everyone she is."

I bit tactfully into the apple I'd brought—until my first paycheque, I would not be partaking of the food court fare—while Renata poked at her dry cubes of lamb souvlaki from La Mediterranée.

"What do you write?" she asked.

"Short stories."

"About what?"

I hated that question. "People," I said.

"Are you published?"

I hated that one even more. I named the literary magazines my stories had appeared in. Their titles made them sound like seed catalogues.

"I have a story for you," she said.

I was probably cringing by then. I never called myself a writer or really thought of myself as one yet. I certainly never imagined that one day I too would pull out of my hat that scabied, half-dead rabbit, the writer-protagonist. Renata must have sensed this because she waved off what she'd said with her plastic fork.

"I guess people tell you that all the time."

We left the food court to join the fray at the photocopy machine, making a quick tour of the shops on our way. Renata stopped at the la Vie en Rose sale rack and held a scrap of red lace against her ample body. There was more tag than panty.

Back in the staff room, she showed me a picture of her kids taped to the wall of her carrel.

Maybe daughters would be better.

"This one's Evelyn. This is Angela."

We settled down to prep. "Moo," I said.

Renata said, "Oh, baby! You're so hard!"

THE STORY I thought Renata wanted to tell me came out during lunch a few weeks later. Once, back when she was studying music at UBC, she overslept. If she took the bus, she'd be late so she decided to hitch. Almost immediately a car pulled over and she got in with her flute and her book bag.

"I'm heading to the university," she told the driver. "Are you going that far?"

"I'll go as far as you want," he told her.

He was middle-aged, white and white-collared. That is, dressed in a shirt and tie.

"But *pas de* pants," Renata said, taking another mouthful of limp, overdressed Caesar salad from Boston Pizza.

I set my coffee down beside my tuffet-sized cinnamon bun from Cinnabon. "You mean he was naked from the waist down?"

"No. He was wearing shoes and socks. Isn't there a law that says you have to wear shoes while driving?"

"Oh my God." I covered my mouth with my hand. Later, thankfully before my next class, I saw in the bathroom mirror four cinnamon-glazed fingerprints on my left cheek. "What happened?"

"The wheel rubbed against his erection as he steered."

"You didn't jump out?"

"No." She crunched a crouton, smirking. "I didn't want to be late for class."

DURING THIS TIME, the early 1990s, there were still cheap apartments in the city. I found one after I got back from Ireland, a pink-applianced studio off Oak Street which I furnished with a Therm-a-Rest pad, a folding IKEA chair, a card table, and a lamp. I had sold all my books when I graduated, except for my two-volume *Oxford English Dictionary* with its accompanying magnifying glass, sturdy enough in its case to be used as an additional item of furniture. Every evening I sat reading in my IKEA chair with my feet up on the *Oxford*, the English language my footrest. My old university friends were lost or scattered. Not that I wanted to go out. I felt too tired most of the time.

I owned one of everything: pot, dish, knife, fork, spoon, cup. Also a cherry pitter that the previous tenant had left behind. I had a computer and printer, of course, and two boxes of story drafts. When I was hired at the college, I'd planned to sneak some file folders, until I saw the inventory posted inside the door of the supply cabinet. I was proud of my austerity. I'd shunned the crass material world in favour of the writing life. At least that was what I hoped, that the paucity of my circumstances was a lifestyle choice, not a physical manifestation of my inner state.

Two and a half years before, I'd left Vancouver with X, the man who'd been in the same fiction workshop as Janine. I won't employ a pseudonym, for that would make him a character and, having taken considerable pains to avoid him up to now, I hardly want to encounter him in this story. Toronto, the literary hub of Canada then as now, was our destination. With my newly acquired MFA, I got hired to teach essay writing at a community college while X started on his novel. I only had weekends and evenings to write, most of which were taken up with marking, lesson planning, and accompanying X to Grossman's Tavern and other legendary drinking holes I'd never heard of. Since I earned more—X was always waiting on a possible grant—I paid the rent and bought the groceries. Every few weeks X would ask for feedback on his writing. Less frequently he would ask to read what I was working on, then tell me my style was too influenced by his. Once he accused me of copying him.

We lived together for a whole year before it occurred to me to save myself. Why I didn't act before this I'm not exactly sure, but I suspect hormones had something to do with it. To effect my plan, I made myself even smaller. I curled into a tiny ball, the way certain animals do in the face of a predator, and simply waited for him to go away. Eventually, though it took a long time, almost another year, X told me that sex with me was boring and that he was moving out, at which point I made straight for the Irish artist colony in case X changed his mind and came back.

WHEN SHE GAVE me this story, Renata said, "But you have to change my name."

"Naturally."

"And what I look like."

"Of course."

"Make me something else. Chinese or Italian."

"How about Jewish? I have serious Jew envy."

"Really?" Her dark eyebrows rose above the frames of her sunglasses. "Why?"

"Read Grace Paley. Then you'll know."

"Better idea," Renata said. "Say I'm dead."

"That would be too sad," I told her.

I never asked what she wanted me to do about the kids.

ONE DAY STERLING came down to lunch. He was medium in every way—height, weight, looks, the brown of his hair. Except for his eyes, which were a pretty, glassy blue, and his complexion, a veritable PSA for the effects of an exclusively fast-food diet, or so his food court choices suggested: dingy more than pallid, jawline sparsely scabbed with razor-beheaded pimples, fingers always feeling under the back of his collar, reading the Braille of acne there.

In the elevator he announced, "The staff room is unfenestrated."

"What does that mean?" Renata asked.

"It doesn't have any windows," I said. Another possible explanation for his dinge.

"Damn it, Charlotte," he said. "*You* should be teaching the TOEFL."

Barely one step ahead of his class, Sterling kept gruellingly long prep hours hunched in his carrel. He'd never joined us for lunch before this because, at the end of the term, his students would be writing the Test of English as a Foreign Language. He said he probably wouldn't pass it should he be forced to take it.

"*Tête-à-tête*? That's not even English," he complained as he wove through the food court tables bearing his Papa Burger and fries on a tray. Kids kept bowing to him and he smiled back even though he despised them.

The three of us found a table. "They already know more grammar than I do," Sterling went on. "They'll pass that test. Then they'll take over the country."

"Now, now," Renata chided.

The only staff member who wasn't white, Renata had her own complaints. She said her students didn't respect her because she was a Canadian-born Chinese who could speak neither Cantonese nor Mandarin. At the same time, they doubted her English, or her ability to teach it. Sometimes, passing her classroom, I saw her standing at the board, tall, athletic, fists pressed to lean hips as she stared down the boys at the back. Her black hair was cut in slashes. With one devastating huff, she blew it out of her eyes. They cowered.

Sterling took a pull of his root beer. "'Inexorable,' 'doppelgänger,' 'solipsistic.' Who uses words like that anyway?"

"Janine used 'inexorable' a while ago," I said.

"I taught it to her," Sterling said.

"You did not." She'd been quoting our creative writing professor who used to urge us to discover the "inexorable endings" to our stories.

"Janine," snorted Renata, who harboured some unarticulated grievance against her, probably involving the photocopier. "She's not a writer. Charlotte's the writer. You should read that story of hers where the wife sews her husband's clothes to the bed."

I turned to Renata. "Where did you read *that*?"

"I went to the library. They have back issues of all those magazines. I read another one too, but that was my favourite. I loved the sexual tension."

Sterling's face pinkened with interest and I saw that, with a little colour in his face, he might actually have been cute.

"Are you sexually tense, Charlotte?" he asked.

I HAD STARTED at the ESL college in the January term. By the summer term Renata and I were good enough friends to see each other outside work. One Sunday we met up at Kits Beach, where she was taking her kids swimming.

Sons? Daughters?

Her sons. The boys hung their heads shyly as she introduced them, yarmulkes bobby-pinned to their curly heads. They had her smile that went too far, revealing first teeth, then a broad pink border of gum. Released off the leash of manners, they sprang up on a driftwood log only to knock each other down again. I felt exhausted just watching them.

We went to put on our bathing suits. The older boy, Evan, wanted to change in the men's room.

"You're not changing in the men's room," Renata said. "You're coming with us."

"We don't need you," both boys said.

"That's what you think."

The younger one, Andrew, said, "We should have put on our bathing suits under our clothes."

"You'll thank me later for providing you with opportunities to look at naked women."

"Yuck!" they screeched as she hustled them inside with us.

I *had* worn my bathing suit under my clothes. Renata took off her T-shirt and bra and began searching in her bag for her suit. By how unhurriedly she went about this, I sensed that she wanted me to see her breasts, tanned the same even brown as her back and arms. The proof is in the details, my creative writing professor used to say. I took out my sunscreen and, with one foot on the bench, applied it assiduously to my knee. Meanwhile, the boys, having locked themselves inside a change stall, began kicking the door.

"Help me," said Renata, lifting the mass of dark curls off her neck. I tied the spaghetti straps of her bikini top. She was hot to the touch.

"Accidents," she said.

"What?"

She glanced at the stall door that seemed to bend outward with each blow. Maybe they weren't kicking it. Maybe they were hurling each other against it.

"Both of them. Unplanned and nine months apart. If I didn't have my tubes tied after Andrew, I'd have ten by now."

The stall door flew open and the little accidents came hurtling out. Renata gathered up their clothes and hers and we left the change room and found a place in the hot sand to lay our towels. Then we waded to our waists in the coliform-brown water while the accidents jumped off the lifeguard float and purposely splashed us with the stuff.

"I was so unprepared to be a mother," Renata told me. "Stuck at home with two babies. I mean, I loved being with them, they're my whole life. But it was mind-numbing."

One day, when the babies were down for a nap and Renata was herself lying in a stupor on the bed, the phone rang. A whisper on the other end, languorous and male: "What are you wearing?"

A few years later call display would force all the obscene callers to retreat like little brown bats or spotted owls. Retreat and wait, for eventually the internet arrived and vastly extended their reach. But before this, they phoned.

"Who is this?" Renata asked the caller.

"An interested party."

That morning she and Gary had quarrelled before he left for work. She'd told him she was bored. He'd said he didn't think boredom was an appropriate emotion for a mother. "We're Jewish, right. It's all about the mother."

Renata actually thought it was Gary phoning to apologize. "Because of the way he said, 'An interested party.' Gary's a lawyer."

She told him: sweatpants and a flannel pajama top mapped with baby spit-up.

"What are you doing?" the caller asked.

"Lying on the bed."

She heard his inhalation, felt herself drawn in.

"Close your eyes," he said.

"They're closed already."

She did what he told her to do and enjoyed it very much.

"It wasn't Gary," I said.

"Of course not. He'd never do a thing like that. He's *so* straitlaced."

"When did you realize it wasn't him?"

She tilted her face to the sun, catlike. "Well before I came."

EMPTY FREIGHTERS IDLED in the bay, doing nothing but displace water. Sailboats plied around them, kayaks cut straight and steady lines, but the inertia of the bigger ships was not to be denied. The girls, in matching sailor-style two-piecers, were already back onshore, building a sand mansion for their Barbies. I yawned and Renata said, "Let's get out."

We left the water and settled side by side in the sand, me sitting with my knees tucked up, Renata leaning back, legs stretched out, propped up on her elbows. She grabbed a handful of her belly flesh and let it go with a snort. Though she was constantly complaining about her weight, hers was the voluptuous fat women hate and men love. It was her Italian birthright. Compared to her, I was ribby and hipless, a *gamine* according to the TOEFL.

"Should I go on?" she asked.

I scooped up sand and let it run through my fingers. In truth, I admired her audacity. But how could she do such a thing without consequences? Emotional consequences.

"Too bad I don't write erotica," I joked.

"Why don't you? I hear it pays."

"Oh, Renata."

"Oh, Charlotte."

"Sex scenes are brutal to write."

"It'd be good for you. Has Sterling asked you out yet?"

"What?" I turned to look at her. She hooked her sunglasses with a finger and pulled them down as far as the bump.

"He asked me for your phone number."

Groaning, I fell back on my towel, shielding my eyes with my arm. "Sterling is so…so…solipsistic."

"He's a doppelgänger," Renata conceded.

"And he's unfenestrated!"

"Still." She rolled over onto her stomach. From under my arm, I peeked at her falling out of her bikini top the way fruit spills from a shopping bag.

"Still what?" I said.

"He's cute in a Dumbo way. You could remake him. Anyway, you don't have to like him."

I swatted at her. Sand got in my eyes and I sat up again, blinking it out. "Did the obscene caller phone again?"

"Every day. Same time."

"Every day? Didn't he have a job?"

"He worked from home."

"How did you find that out?"

She lowered herself off one elbow, then the other, settling a cheek on her folded arms. "I got to know him pretty well."

THROUGH THEIR WRITING, Grace Paley, Cynthia Ozick, Philip Roth, Nathanael West et al. felt like intimates. But I'd never had an in-the-flesh Jewish friend before. I loved the Yiddish words Renata sprinkled over her sentences. Some frantic riffling of dictionaries must have gone on in her class. What are "nosh," "schmooze," and "schnozzle" in Japanese, Mandarin, and Korean? I was just an Anglican girl from Calgary. I didn't have a culture.

"Is it true there's a light bulb in the handkerchief?"

"That would be one cheap wedding," Renata said.

I said I wanted to try gefilte.

"What's gee-filt?"

"You know. Gefilte fish."

"Ah!" she shrieked. "If you only knew how funny you are!"

I still wore clothes my mother passed on to me at Christmas. Renata got down on her knees in the staff room and stapled the hem of my skirt above my knees. She opened the second button on my blouse.

I wondered what she wanted from me besides a story that, if I actually wrote it and it actually got published, would be read by, at most, fifty people. Because she'd given up music when she had children, maybe my accomplishments, modest though they were, met her standard for vicariousness. But later she told me she'd never been good enough to pursue a career in music.

I asked why she didn't give her story to Janine.

"Janine is a schmuck," she said.

It was true that I was not a schmuck. Some of the people at the school were. Some, like Sterling, were not quite as sharp as the tack waiting on their chair. This, in addition to his attitude toward his students, was why I didn't want to go out with him. Yet the afternoon he surprised me by lunging halfway over the wall our two carrels made and asking me, I said yes. I can't explain why when ever since Renata had warned me of his interest, I'd been avoiding him to forestall the moment of my inexorable refusal. I said yes but meant no, because I couldn't seem to uncurl myself and say it. I had started on iron supplements and made an appointment to have my thyroid checked as well. The iron hadn't kicked in yet.

That night, I called Renata for advice. "Charlotte," she said. "How will you ever become a writer if you have no passion?"

This was exactly what X told me when he left me.

"You can't be serious," I said.

"Sometimes when you're in a rut, or, I don't know, depressed? Doing something different can snap you out of it. Something out of character."

"Sterling has buboes on the back of his neck," I told her.

"What are buboes?" Renata asked.

DURING THE TIME of the phone calls, Renata's in-laws came over from Hong Kong for an extended visit. She said to her mother-in-law, "I have a doctor's appointment."

And the next week, "I'm taking an exercise class."

Also, "I really appreciate you taking the babies for a few hours."

This was after she'd asked to meet him.

"Um," he said on the phone. "Where? No, I can't."

"You live alone? Then how about your place?"

"No. Um. Better not."

He sounded different than when he commanded her to roll over, to get onto her knees, to bind various parts of her body with the phone cord. In ordinary conversation, he was a disappointment. "It was like seeing a picture of a sexy radio announcer and thinking, Who's the fat guy?"

"But you didn't know what he looked like."

"Not yet, but I knew then what he *was* like. I could hear his knees knocking together."

She suggested they meet in a café. Just to talk. "Near your place," she told him. "I don't have all day."

He lived in the West End. "Where all the fun happens," Renata said. She chose a seat from which she could see and be seen. When he walked in, she knew him right away.

"How?" I asked.

"Shifty."

"Did he know you?"

"He walked right past me. Because I'm Asian. And I was wearing my glasses instead of my contacts. Not a sexy look."

He took a seat facing the door. Every time a woman entered, he blushed. After about ten minutes, his gaze ping-ponging from watch to door, he looked over at Renata.

"And?"

"I realized why he liked the phone. Every dirty little thought was written on his face."

He pointed, mouthed: *you?* She huffed, clearing her black fringe. He had to obey her then.

"I thought we were going to talk," he said, following her out.

She said, "Haven't we talked enough?"

ON SATURDAY NIGHT at exactly the time we'd agreed to meet at the movie theatre, I phoned Sterling and left a message on his answering machine saying I was sick. I *was* sick. All weekend, both before and after making the call, my stomach churned. I lay balled on the bed, feverish with guilt. It was impossible for me to go to the movie with him. If I did, I would have to go for a drink afterward. I would not be able to say no. Then he would start coming down for lunch in the food court all the time. He'd ask me out again the next weekend, maybe for dinner or a party. This would lead—inexorably again, for all my nos came out as yeses!—to me sleeping with him and consequently falling in love even though I didn't even like him. I knew this because it had happened before, most recently with X, who'd been arrogant and dismissive of everyone in our workshop, including me, until I slept with him. After I slept with him, his arrogance seemed misperceived. How had I judged him so harshly when he was so obviously wonderful? But he wasn't wonderful, or different in any way. I was different. One surge of oxytocin and I lost myself. By the time I'd realized it, I was stuck.

Having decided never to go back to the college, I spent Sunday preparing my resumé.

On Monday, a bullying sense of responsibility drove me into work. I couldn't just not show up. Someone would have to cover my classes, probably Renata. As luck would have it, Sterling was for once not huddled in his carrel, but at the photocopy machine, hand deep in its guts. I went right over.

"Did you get my message, Sterling? I threw up all weekend. I'm still nauseated."

The latter was a fact.

In a crouch, face contorting, he strained to reach the jam. I hovered above him, pleading with the part in his hair. "I'm really, really sorry. Was it good?"

I heard a ripping sound. He drew out a corner of paper, sprang up, kicked the machine.

"Fuck off!"

He didn't look at or speak to me again for the remaining

six weeks that I worked there. I should have been grateful for this but, in truth, it bothered me a lot. If the room was hot, Sterling's anger made it so. If it was cold, it was due to his contempt. Though the other teachers treated me with the same collegial indifference as before, I couldn't help thinking that Sterling had said something to them. After a couple of miserable days, I mailed off my resumé.

A week later Mrs Armstrong, the vice-principal, called me into her office. She was usually seen sailing the halls, D-cups thrust forward, her own figurehead. I had no trouble picturing Sterling sobbing between those solid cones.

"Sit down, Charlotte," she said, gesturing to the hot seat that faced her cluttered desk.

On the wall behind her, calligraphic scrolls and posters in Chinese advertised the school, the same ones probably pasted on light posts all over Taipei and Hong Kong. A pair of framed degrees informed me that Barbara Elaine Armstrong and I shared an alma mater, thirty years apart, and that she'd also gone to business school. I tried to remember Sterling's last name because it suddenly occurred to me that Mrs Armstrong might be his mother.

"I assume you know what this is about," she said.

I did. She was going to fire me for standing Sterling up.

"This is a private college. I know you worked previously in a public institution where they are free to put everything on the taxpayer's tab. Here we run a business accountable to a board of directors. Who could possibly require twenty-six pieces of chalk? Eight boxes of paper clips? Are you making necklaces? The attendance books should do for several terms. You've been here three terms and taken twelve books."

"I didn't."

"They're not scribblers, you know."

"I've taken maybe six pieces of chalk."

She passed a paper over the desk to me. "Are these your initials?"

According to the inventory I had initialled for all these things. "I didn't take them."

"They're gone! Who took them?"

"I have no idea," I lied.

In the end, she believed me and said she would bring up the matter at the next staff meeting. She apologized for accusing me of something I hadn't done and promised to get to the bottom of it.

The next day I stayed late to prep and, alone in the staff room, made five photocopies of my 197-page manuscript. I also took and initialled for the 12 × 18 manila envelopes.

THE GIRLS WANTED ice cream so we rose and brushed away the sand sunscreen had glued to us. I shook out my towel and, while Renata merely hung her beach bag over one muscled shoulder and glided on, lithe and bikinied, I tripped along beside her, clutching my towel around me. Evelyn and Angela flip-flopped ahead, peach-like buttocks wiggling under their sailor skirts. So coquettish at such a young age.

"Your story's like *Belle de Jour*," I told Renata in the concession line. "Did you see it? With Catherine Deneuve?"

"A Chinese Catherine Deneuve? Nice! Or should I be insulted that you just called me a prostitute?"

I was shocked that she would say this with the girls right there.

"Who was the director again?" she asked.

"Buñuel." I got an idea then about how this story might actually work. "Have you seen *That Obscure Object of Desire*? The one where two actresses play the same character?"

Renata pushed the black spikes out of her eyes. "No."

"They don't even look the same," I said.

"Sounds confusing."

"Only at first."

The concession line advanced us to the counter. "What do you want, Evie? Angie?"

"You'd like it," I said. "It's perverted."

"Shhh," she said, gesturing to the girls.

RENATA AND HER pervert walked a few blocks to where an older building squatted between two high-rises.

"Was he ugly?" I asked.

"Not at all. A little thin on top. An irregular shaver and not the cleanest person in the world, but that was hardly a surprise."

"Teeny-weeny?"

"Average."

Then why, I wondered. Why, if he was a presentable person, not maimed or hideous, if he could go out and meet women or answer personal ads, which were at that time published in, of all places, the newspaper, there being at that time, newspapers—why did he feel the need to call complete strangers and say dirty things to them?

"Can you tell me his name?" I asked.

"You've got to change it."

"I'll change it."

But I think I won't name him either. He's not important.

I asked what he did. "For a living, I mean!"

"Technical writer. Textbooks and manuals, though he was also working on a screenplay. Who isn't? Have you written a screenplay, Charlotte?"

"What was his place like?"

"A sty. Papers and dishes everywhere. He smoked and butted out on the plates."

The girls had finished their ice cream and were playing out of earshot with their Barbies again, redeveloping the mansion.

"You really had sex?" I whispered.

She nodded.

"But what about Gary? What about the girls?"

"What about them? They had nothing to do with it."

"But how could you just go over to this stranger's apartment and have sex? He could have given you a disease. He could have murdered you."

We were lying on our backs again, side by side, by then. She lifted an arm and traced a languid arc. I had no idea what it meant.

"Did you see him again?"

"Lots when the in-laws were here. It was more difficult after that. I got worried too, that Gary would find out. In the end, I unlisted our number."

"How did you explain that to Gary?"

"I told him about the calls. He was appalled."

I was still trying to process all she'd said when she changed the subject and her tone. Gone, the obvious pleasure she'd taken in scandalizing me.

"What happened to you, Charlotte?"

"What do you mean?" I asked.

I knew what she meant. What had curled me into this tight,

prudish ball? And I wondered then—was any of it true? Couldn't she have been trying, Scheherazade-like, to get *me* to talk?

"Nothing," I told her.

I COULDN'T TELL her. More exactly, I couldn't find the words, despite the fact that I'd pledged myself to a life of them. That hot summer afternoon in Toronto, when we both put aside our writing because X wanted to make love?—I didn't understand it, so how could I speak of it? He wanted to make love and so we did, and once we started, I got into it too. So much that, afterward, as I lay half asleep, swathed in the muggy air, groggy with bliss, I wanted more. He sat up; I held him back. It seemed he would oblige me. He smiled, bent, nudged. I opened my legs. I opened myself. I gave everything to him, including my trust, until the moment he bit down hard.

Nothing, nothing I have experienced before or since, hurt as much as that.

A FEW WEEKS after I sent out my resumé, I got a call from the community college. They interviewed me for the sub list, but then a new infusion of government money for immigrant language training came in and I was hired to teach a night class. It was for more pay, and unionized too. Also, it gave me the whole day to write.

I only saw Renata once more after that, though we talked regularly on the phone.

"I hate you," she said. "How could you leave me here?"

"What did you have for lunch?"

"Nippon Express. It's not the same without you, Charlotte. Come back."

"Get on the sub list here, Renata."

"And work nights? I want to see my kids. Besides, I don't have a certificate, remember?"

She said management had moved the supply cupboard into the office. Mrs Armstrong personally distributed the supplies. "You have to stop on the way to the bathroom and perform a trick for toilet paper."

We laughed about that, then I slipped in that my book had been accepted. "A friend recommended me to his publisher. It happened so fast."

"Oh Charlotte! That's fantastic! Am I in it?"

"I tried, Renata. I just couldn't get it right."

At Christmas she and Evelyn and Angela took me to *The Nutcracker* because Gary couldn't make it. In the Ladies before the performance, she and the girls primped. She let them wear lipstick because it was a special occasion. "Put some on too, Charlotte. Live a little."

She took a step back, fluffing her hair in the mirror, then smoothing her knit dress. "Whenever I touch my stomach," she said, "I think of panettone."

It was Janine who called me in February with the news.

"What are you talking about?" I shrieked.

"Don't shout at me."

"She isn't even forty! She has two kids!"

"Apparently there was something the matter with her heart."

*

AT THE MEMORIAL service a photograph of Renata laughing stood on the altar—if that's what it's called in a synagogue. Friends and relatives I didn't know came up to speak. What a wonderful wife, daughter, mother, sister, friend she was, an accomplished musician, a gifted teacher. No one said she was sexy or funny or audacious—the very traits that defined her for me, her constants—and the stories were all different from the ones Renata had told me. As I sat there making a mess of my wet tissue, rolling bits of it into worms, I felt as though the defective heart in yet other Renata had given out. And I wondered about death, an even greater mystery than sex.

Afterward there was a reception in the basement. The family stood in the vestibule to accept condolences. During the service I'd been sitting in a rear pew, unable to figure out the back of which yarmulked head belonged to Gary. Now I found myself standing before him in the black dress my mother had sent by Canada Post, self-consciousness my only accessory since Renata wasn't there to fix me up. I was so flustered I could hardly speak. It wasn't only what I knew and he did not that made the moment awkward. We are all attracted to a type and he was mine—dark and full-lipped, with Heathcliff eyes. How could she have done it, I wondered. How could she have betrayed so gorgeous and loyal a man? A man with a sexy dimple in his chin that Renata, astonishingly, had not even bothered to mention. I stared right at it, fighting the urge to rise up on my toes and place the tip of my tongue in it.

I stammered my name. Gary seized my hand and enclosed it in a warm, long-fingered squeeze. "Thank you. Thank you for coming. Renata talked so much about you. She was excited about your book."

My hand cupped in his. I pictured him bringing it to his lips and blowing on it and me coming back to life.

"She talked about you too," I said, face heating up.

"She said you were writing a story about her."

"I never finished it. I couldn't get the ending right."

"If you ever do, I hope you'll show it to me."

"I will," I said, and he let go of my hand. It felt cold, bereft, as though it didn't have a mate. I started crying again and turned to the next person in line. There were the accidents, orphans now, fidgeting beside their dad.

"Your mother loved you so much," I sobbed as they took turns stoically shaking my hand.

I had come to the funeral with Janine and another teacher from the school, Sophie. I washed my face in the bathroom, then, spotting the beacon of Janine's hair in the crowd, joined them.

"God, it's just so sad," Janine was telling Sophie. They had already helped themselves to sandwiches.

I stood watching for Gary to come into the room, not so I could speak to him. I just wanted to look at him. It was perverse, I knew, to have cried so much over Renata and now to be so attracted to her husband. It was some kind of transference, I decided, and forced myself to turn my back to the door.

"I didn't know she played the flute," Sophie said.

"She was so talented," Janine said. "We were fortunate to have known her."

What a schmuck, I thought, and stalked off to the refreshment table.

In the story I had got as far as Renata breaking it off with her lover. I didn't know where to go from there. What were the repercussions? Would Gary find out? No. I didn't ever want him to know. Then how would I end the story? How would Renata want it to end? I put a lettuce-ruffled triangle on my plate and found a corner to be alone in. Just then, Sterling walked in. Mouth open, the sandwich halfway to it, I met his glassy-blue gaze. And he raised a palm in the air, solemn and unsmiling, offering peace.

It came to me then, my ending, surprising and inexorable.

I watched him fill his plate then cross over to Sophie and Janine. When I joined them a minute later, they weren't talking about Renata anymore, but about the school. I waited for the moment when Sterling, nervous in my presence, would disengage. Sophie and Janine continued chatting. He fell silent, brushed the corners of his mouth with the back of his hand, then used his pinkie nail to dredge between his front teeth. I hadn't noticed his teeth before, white and wide-spaced, a child's teeth. The acned neck was an old familiar sight, of course. The poor guy had no one to squeeze his pimples for him.

"I didn't see you upstairs," I said, touching his arm.

He looked, not at me, but at my hand holding on too long. His biceps tensed. I felt it swell and knew he was wondering what was up.

Salacity, prurience, concupiscence.

Did he even know the meaning of these words? Did he understand that when I gave him my saddest smile and said, "Take me home?" I intended to ask him in.

He stayed the night, but I never saw him again after that.

FROM THE ARCHIVES
OF THE HOSPITAL FOR THE INSANE

MARGARET C. (#1506) happened to be passing through the main foyer when Matron Fillmore ushered the new girl into the superintendent's office. A tall woman accompanied them, also nicely turned out. From her agonized expression, Margaret guessed her to be the mother. The girl herself Margaret put in the class of the half dead, for they were either admitted like that or came in a blaze of life. So thin, this one, with stones for eyes.

Feet aching, she limped on to the linens room. Camphor and iron scorch. *The care of the bedding and linen shall rest with the Matron, and she shall see to the careful use of articles of every kind* ... Each folded piece of mending Margaret unloaded from her basket and placed on the returned pile for Matron to inventory. *She shall keep a record of all property in the Hospital, with additions and alterations made therein from time to time* ... Since her own arrival nearly five years earlier, Margaret had handsewn 1,220 articles of clothing for both male and female patients, as well as thirty-six restraining camisoles. She had, furthermore, mended 15,640 pieces and though these included sheets, towels, tablecloths, bed ticks, and the like, each reminded her that the material body itself was a kind of garment, a garment for the spirit.

She thought back to the new girl. Tight waists were ever the fashion, yet her dress had hung on her as though no one was inside it.

Luncheon followed. Beetroot salad, potted ham, lemon pudding. Bread and butter. Tea or lemonade. *A separate dish shall always be used for dessert. Spoons shall be supplied with sauce and pudding.*

In the dining room, Margaret shared a table with pug-eyed Augusta W. (#1782), who believed her husband planned to sell her to Chinamen. She would speak of nothing else, but often only brooded on it, which was the case today. Across sat Bertha H. (#3388), who'd arrived the previous month under police escort, dishevelled and screeching out names of prominent political men who'd purchased her favours. Off she went to the isolation annex, the squat tower behind Lawn House that everyone called "the octagon." She was back now and her broad face, scrubbed of paint, looked younger for it, though probably not as young as it really was; the oldest profession, Margaret had observed here, aged the practitioner. She longed to ask who Bertha had seen, or heard, in the octagon, but judging by her droopy, bromided look, now was not the time.

Also at the table: Freda T. of the flaming hair (#2592), who'd tried to smother her week-old baby; Julia M. (#3299), who knew no English; Rosa J. (#1569), her pink tongue jutting.

As she ate, just as while she worked, Margaret directed her thoughts toward that better world. She was a New Church believer, a congregant of one, though that would change if ever she left here or, obviously, when she found herself on the other side. For now, her understanding of her faith came from a pamphlet taken away from her when she arrived, the gist of which had been that everyone was born for heaven and if they didn't end up there, it was on account of poor conduct in this world. Love and be useful, serve others. One day Margaret would shed this heavy raiment of flesh and join the angels. Why, she'd be one herself! This was exactly what she'd promised Lucy L. (#3019).

Margaret glanced around the dining room for the new girl, prematurely she knew. After admission, patients went to the observation dormitory. Pricked, questioned, relieved of their belongings, then issued hospital garb, they stayed there at least a week. The girl might even end up over in Lawn House in her own clothes, though by the deadened look in her eye, Margaret doubted it.

*

HOSPITALS FOR INSANE ACT
Form C (Section 7(c) and Section 20)

Statement to be forwarded to the Medical Superintendent when Application is Made for the Reception of a Patient

1. Name of patient . . . *Helen H.*
2. Where from . . . *Vancouver*
3. Sex and age last birthday . . . *Female – 19*
4. State as to Marriage . . . *Single*
5. Occupation of patient (or that of husband or father) . . .
   Father a druggist. Patient employed by him as a sometime clerk.

6. Habits in health – as to temperance, industry, and general conduct, etc. . . . *Good health generally, but over-particular with food. Prone to fancies. The patient's mother complains of excess novel-reading.*

7. Education . . . *Good*

8. Religion . . . *Methodist*

9. Insanity, how manifested . . . *State of extreme apathy. Gaze fixed, though she does not appear to hear voices. Emaciated.*

10. Where previously treated . . . *Burrard Sanitarium. While in B.S., she underwent an ovariectomy.*

11. Relatives similarly affected . . . *None reported, though the patient's mother has, in the opinion of this doctor, neurosis writ large upon her forehead.*

12. Appetite for food . . . *Poor*

13. Any faltering of speech or loss of power and when . . . *Will not speak.*

14. What delusions . . . *According to her mother, she believes that she has brought disgrace upon the family.*

15. Whether suicidal (attempted or threatened) . . . *Yes. Swallowed bichloride of mercury and laudanum.*

16. Whether dangerous to others, how . . . *No*

17. Other particulars . . . *Mother says the patient became amorously obsessed with an employee of her father. His dismissal aroused the patient's congenital inclinations. She was admitted some weeks later to the B.S. The family removed her after three months. A suicide attempt followed.*

I certify to the best of my knowledge that the above particulars are correctly stated; and I hereby request you receive

the above-mentioned ... *Helen H.* .... whom I last saw at ...
St. Paul's Hospital ... on the ... *2nd* ... of ... *August, 1908* ...
as a patient of unsound mind, and a patient in the ... *New Westminster Asylum.*

Name: E. B. Bayfield, MD
Address: Vancouver

*

TEN DAYS AFTER the girl's arrival, Margaret sat hemming in her shared room in C Ward, its white walls and floors scrubbed by the three others who currently slept there—Rosa J. of the jutting tongue, Julia M. of the foreign tongue, and Freda T., driven mad by her baby's cries. Lucy L.'s help, when she'd been here, hadn't been worth the effort to enlist. As for Margaret, she was too crippled now for physical work beyond that accomplished while seated. Her slippers had to be slit to accommodate her bunions, which were but one torment. The burn and ache across her soles made a glass-strewn path of every floor.

C Ward housed resistive, incurable, chronic, and suicidal females. About two years ago, Matron Fillmore suggested Margaret move from these often-chaotic quarters. In Lawn House, the newer annex, she would enjoy homier rooms and the company of less-afflicted women.

"Plenty of patients rid themselves of false beliefs after a rest at Lawn House," Matron had said. "Just last week one lady confessed that she'd only imagined all those terrors. She was so glad to be there. In a month or two she'll be discharged back to her husband."

Though long inured to slights against her faith, Margaret couldn't help shuddering over this woman's fate. She explained to Matron that it would be too long a hobble from Lawn House to the main building to collect and drop off her work. What neither voiced was how, in addition to her industrious needle, Margaret, a calm presence amidst C Ward's turmoil, was often more helpful with troublesome patients than the attendants, who were not proper nurses either.

She tied off the thread and, reaching for her scissors on the sill, glanced out the window. Fixed shut, it overlooked the front grounds. *All patients who are not otherwise healthfully employed should walk out twice daily in suitable weather* ... Nearly two hundred patients milled about the vast lawn, shooed along by attendants. They formed two groups ... *Male and female walking-parties must not be permitted to mingle* ..., women in pale gingham dresses, bonnets, and aprons, and the men, the great majority, in coarser unbleached duck. Beyond, the Fraser River pushed its silty brown current in the same desultory manner. Only the unmistakable Rosa flitted about in the August heat. Was she chasing a bee? In body Rosa was possibly twenty, in brain four, which was also her approximate height in feet.

Margaret started on a new piece from her basket, only to be distracted when a commotion broke out. Rosa howling, attendants rushing to her. Some patients began wailing along, mockingly, or because their own derangements had been set off. She paused to watch the C Ward day attendant, a middle-aged woman with a face like a strongbox, marching the bawling Rosa across the grass in the direction of the front entrance. Newish, she'd replaced the uppity attendant who'd quit over Lucy.

Before long, Rosa, bonnet lost along the way, was roughly deposited with Margaret without a word from the grim attendant, who immediately departed. Rosa came sniffling over, slanted eyes wet with tears. Tongue out as always. As always, Margaret longed to poke it with her needle, and might have, if not for the angels. Instead, when Rosa extended her child's hand to show Margaret the crimson welt, Margaret remembered her purpose was to love and kissed it.

Matron Fillmore brought in the new girl then, dressed now in gingham. *The effect of being in so novel a place, where the doors are locked and the windows guarded, is to make many patients apprehensive of harm, and their fears should be quieted ... Make them feel that they have come among friends ...* Matron made her cheerful introductions, avoiding Margaret's eye. She had that broad accent of the Maritimes, though the girl, whose name was Helen, gave no sign of hearing anything Matron said.

"This is a quiet room, Helen. You'll soon feel better here."

Shown to Lucy's former bed by the door, Helen H. (#3396) promptly lay down and tucked herself into a tight, kittenish ball.

Before leaving, Matron finally graced Margaret with a look. Sharp nose, lips turned in to prevent smiling—a hawk's face. Yet those pellet eyes had communicated many a preemptive thank-you in the past for making a new patient feel welcome; now they narrowed under the starched pouf of her cap. A warning, or a reminder of their stalemate over Lucy? Margaret had not directly refuted her involvement in the affair, because in good conscience she couldn't lie. In turn, Matron wouldn't tell her where Lucy had ended up.

As soon as Matron left, Rosa crept over to the bed that was now Helen's. "Wha-wha-wha's matter?"

Again, no response from the girl. Maybe she spoke some gibbery tongue, like Julia M. According to the story circulating C Ward, Julia had been betrothed to a countryman who'd settled over on Vancouver Island, but on her way to join him, had been struck with a fit. Pulled frothing from the train, she was brought first to the Kamloops hospital, then here. Whoever the man was, he was unlikely to claim an epileptic wife. Deportation would be Julia's fate once her kin were found.

Margaret would pry a word out of the girl just to know if she spoke English. She set down her work and, rising to knobbed feet, limped over.

Helen's hair, half-undone from its loose bun, resembled a honeyed peony. When Margaret placed a hand on her shoulder, she abruptly rolled onto her back. There they were, the stone-crammed sockets, mouth open, dark with her scream.

"Don't touch me don't touch me don't touch me do not touch!"

Margaret retreated, again thinking of Lucy. She'd screamed too, though more from outrage than terror.

*

NO ONE EXPECTED anything of Helen on her first day on the ward. Instead of working, she lay in her fetal curl until dinner. Margaret stitched in silence, as she would have if alone. Periodically, she broke her meditations to glance over at the unmoving heap across the room.

Patients are to come and go to the dining-rooms together, and the knives and forks are to be gathered up and counted before they leave ... Helen had to be escorted by the attendant, screaming the whole way. Once seated at the next table to Margaret's, she merely stared at her plate, disheveled hair an empty nest on her head.

Fried fish, boiled potatoes, boiled French beans. Canned peaches. Tea or lemonade.

Some patients will go to the table and sit through the meal but not eat, and unless watched it will not be discovered that they are starving themselves. Some can be coaxed to eat. Some have to be fed by the attendant ... By the time the rest of them had finished and were filing out, depositing their cutlery in the basin the box-faced attendant held, Helen had still not touched her food. The attendant set down the basin and began rolling up her sleeves.

Sometime later, Helen returned on her own to C Ward and resumed her balled position on the bed. The rest of them were taking down their hair for the night. Freda's fell in bronzed waves. With her jade-flecked eyes, she might have been beautiful had her husband not kicked out a good number of her teeth.

"Hello you," Freda greeted Helen. When Helen didn't reply, she turned to Margaret. "Where's she from?"

"She won't speak except to tell you not to touch her."

Freda winced.

Before attending to her own coarse tresses, Margaret helped with Rosa's, fine and wheaten-coloured. She combed, shook them by the ends, then gathered the sheaves to be crisscrossed into loose sleeping braids. Wherever Julia came from, they didn't air the roots. She simply fashioned a fresh yellow rope which, during the day, she wore wrapped around her head. Margaret thought of Lucy, whose curls had been so resistant to the comb. What lively screeches they'd provoked!

The day attendant barked in at them, "Your turn, ladies. Look smart. Helen to the tub."

All patients are to be bathed at least weekly, unless exception is made by a physician ... They collected their towels and washcloths. When Helen didn't move, the attendant entered and proceeded to drag her off the bed by her oxters, Helen screaming until she was set upon her feet.

Freda and Margaret exchanged a glance as their silent procession headed for the WC, Rosa scampering ahead, Julia next, towering over Rosa, her back broad and seeming straighter with the plumb line of the yellow braid hanging down it. Freda, then Helen, whose hair, still up, looked now like the seedhead of some jungly sort of plant. As always, Margaret brought up the rear, sliding her feet more than stepping.

She washed herself at the row of basins alongside the others. Face, neck, between her bosoms. An old woman stared back from the mirror, hair and complexion the colour of used bathwater, eyes pale blue. She was fifty-one now, yet still unspectacled, which had to be some kind of miracle.

Her gaze shifted beyond her own reflection to the open bathroom door behind her where the attendant was bent over the tub. *Always turn the cold water on first, and see that the bath and water are clean and of right temperature before the patient gets in* ... Helen finished undressing. Breasts that would barely fill a teacup. And there seemed no flesh at all on the arms that reached behind her to unfasten the button on her drawers. When these dropped, Margaret flinched at what she saw: a concave stomach across which a broad purple smile was carved.

She'd seen the same ghoulish smile in years gone by, but not recently. Poor Lilli S. (#2571), artist of the chamber pot. Trying to cure her of this filthy habit, they'd removed her female organs.

Imagine doing that to a young woman. It should have been a crime.

*

AT 6:30 P.M., the night attendant replaced the one with the steel mouth. Cherub-faced, cap a little askew—from sleeping on the job, they knew for a fact. *Night-watches shall go very quietly about, making as little disturbance as possible, wear slippers or noiseless shoes through the wards, and if doors creak in opening they shall see that this is remedied ... They shall lock all doors admitting to the building ...* She gave Julia her hypodermic in case a fit tossed her to the floor during the night, Julia placidly submitting. By the time the attendant pulled the dark blinds down against the dawdling summer light, Margaret had finished her prayers for Lucy. Clutching the bed frame, she hoisted herself to a stand.

During the day, they dispersed themselves throughout the hospital buildings and grounds according to the work schedule. *The minds of patients must be drawn away and diverted from their morbid thoughts by every available means, and especially by appropriate employment, which will occupy them healthfully and pleasantly ...* But at night, thinking was all there was. Their miseries rushed back, concentrating in these locked rooms, thickening in the hot, fusty air.

In this room, only drugged Julia was spared. Rosa, long ago abandoned here, tossed and whimpered, still wondering why. Freda heaved sleepless sighs for her children, five in all, including the hungry infant whose cries she'd tried to stifle, all boarded out to strangers now. Margaret fretted over Lucy. And from more distant corridors came sobs, shrieks, and sometimes chilly bursts of laughter, or breaking glass that tomorrow would bring the glazier back. Across the hall, someone—it must have been Bertha—began crooning a suggestive song. Her roommates yelled, then the pretty night attendant added to the racket.

"Quiet down, the lot of you! Please!"

Margaret rolled onto her side and, pulling the pillow over her head, turned her thoughts to heaven. This way she might visit it in her dreams once sleep came, the way Julia might be back now with her own people. It sometimes happened. Margaret would find herself in that busy place, sewing of course, her needle made of gold, her thread something rarer than silk. Perhaps she'd pluck out her own hairs and sew with them because she'd be an angel herself then and wouldn't have these wires springing from her head.

Rosa's voice intruded. "Wha-wha-wha's matter?"

Margaret pushed herself to a seated position. In the next bed, Helen was weeping.

"What's wrong, dear?" Margaret whispered across to her.

And Helen finally spoke. "I'm going…"

She was going nowhere, but Margaret humoured her. "Where? Where are you going, dear?"

Where had Lucy gone? Out that upstairs window, then she ran into the night. Everyone on C Ward had helped, even Augusta, whose puggy face Lucy had punched. They helped her because, in addition to her spiritedness, Lucy had been so young, fifteen, the same age as many a daughter and sister. Though Margaret had neither of these, she'd had her purpose. This was no place for a child.

Rosa slid out of bed and skittered over to Helen's side, tongue out, staring at her shaking shoulders. Freda rose next, then Margaret. The three of them gathered round the bed that had been that feral girl's.

"What is it?" Freda murmured. "Maybe we can help."

Eyes closed, head thrashing, Helen seemed to be reliving some terror that may or may not have taken place. Plenty here lived in a phantasmagoria. Horses ran circles on the lawn, their tails set on fire. The sugar bowl was poisoned. Disembodied voices commanded them—Run! Strike! Disrobe! Or they were Queen Alexandra, or Mary, Mother of God. Margaret was beyond surprise, or so she thought until Helen said, "I'm going to have a child."

She pictured the girl's scar. She'd seen bracelets of stitches, a bruise necklace—suicide's adornments. Had Helen done that to *herself*?

"How far along are you?" Freda asked the distraught girl.

No reply.

"When did it happen?"

"What?"

"*It*," Freda said.

And Margaret grimaced, thinking of Lloyd after so long. In heaven, love between the sexes is chaste, of the mind not the body, which opens with supreme pleasure, as does the heart. Lloyd had a mind like a honey bucket. But she wouldn't have to be married to him in heaven even if he somehow bullied his way in.

"February." Helen began to sob again.

Six months ago. Lucy had just arrived.

"Rosa," Freda said. "Back to bed now."

Freda led her by the hand, waiting while Rosa slid the chamber pot out and squatted, then used the bed frame to monkey herself up. Freda covered her and kissed her forehead, a flat extension of her little face. Her mothering redirected to this unlucky, unloved runt. Just like that, Rosa began to snore.

In tactful whispers, Margaret and Freda resumed their questioning.

"Did you know him?"

"Yes. It was Dugal…Dugal McBain."

"And he is?"

"He delivers…delivered…prescriptions for my father."

"You were forced?" Freda was thinking of Helen's screams, Margaret knew.

Helen nodded, then blurted, "But I love him! They sent me away once already. To fix it so I wouldn't have it. But I lay very still, like my sister did with hers. She lost two babies before one finally took."

"Are you sure about the timing?" Freda asked. "You should be showing well by now."

Though darkness was finally overtaking dusk, Margaret could make out the glint of conviction in Helen's eyes. Solemnly, she nodded.

Freda patted Helen's hand. "Tomorrow we'll talk again. Try to sleep now."

*

MARGARET DID NOT visit heaven in her dreams that night, for she didn't dream. She lay awake thinking about that other troubled girl. Lucy L.—sturdy, freckle-spattered, coal scuttle for a mouth. Though expelled from a convent orphanage somewhere in the interior, she adamantly denied a lack of kin. She'd seen her parents' wedding picture, held for safekeeping, just as Lucy herself had been kept safe after her mother died birthing her. Her father, a blacksmith, moved on to look for work, but he was going to come back for her, probably when she turned eighteen.

Great consideration, patience, and forbearance is at all times most essential in dealing with the insane, and attendants are admonished to take no notice of the insulting or offensive language or acts of a patient …

"Satan is that child's father," the day attendant at the time had told Matron Fillmore, loud enough for all to hear.

Lucy was put to work like everyone, first to the kitchen, where she spat in the food, then the laundry, where she punched Augusta for her silly talk. Uproar followed her. Sewing might keep her from the restraining chair.

"You have to sit still to sew," Matron told Margaret. "How are you going to get her to do that?"

Margaret asked to try.

And so Lucy stayed behind with Margaret after the room had been scrubbed and the others had left. "Come close," Margaret told her. "Careful, the floor's wet."

Lucy lifted her skirts to her knees, took two running steps, and with a laugh, slid over to the window and plunked herself down on the end of Julia's bed. The lesson began.

"Didn't the nuns teach you needlework?" Margaret soon had to ask, for even a simple running stitch daunted the girl, her seam as crooked as her mouth and peppered from finger pricks, each of which had prompted a carillon of shrill screams.

"I stabbed an ass-faced boy I hated and didn't have to after that."

Though often seized by the same compulsion, Margaret tutted.

Lucy raised her eyebrows and leaned in. "That was one of the nicer things I did. But I didn't know they'd bloody ship me here, did I? Where'll they send me after this place?"

Margaret pointed out the window, toward the squat octagon behind Lawn House. "See that tower? It's the isolation annex."

Lucy slumped over her work. "I'll be buggered if I'm stuck in this stink hole for three years."

"Be nice and behave. It will keep you in good stead, and not just for now. Through eternity, too."

"What's *that* supposed to mean?"

She told Lucy then of the world on the other side, where the angels lived just like them, in angel houses in angel towns and cities, with streets and parks, almost the same as in our world except everything was beautiful and good. They busied themselves all day, doing God's work.

"What kind of work?" Lucy asked, sucking a finger.

"What each is best at. Some raise children who have crossed over. Some help the ones just waking from death."

Lucy perked up momentarily, perhaps thinking of her dead mother. But then she grumbled, "Work, work, work. Sounds like here. If it is, I'll be buggered if I'm going."

"Don't say that! Think what you're suited for."

"Vaudeville."

This flummoxed Margaret. Vaudeville wasn't mentioned in the tract the New Church woman on the streetcar gave her. Lucy, meanwhile, began an animated recounting of the time she'd escaped the convent and snuck into a show in town. The bag-punching sisters impressed her most. She leapt up and, fists swinging, galumphed about with a huge freckled grin while Margaret laughed and laughed.

"That's what I want to do. Or work at Woodward's dressed up all pretty. Do they have department stores?"

Again, Margaret hesitated. If you had everything you needed, what use would stores be? She seized on the dresses.

"On the other side, you wear garments according to your inner state. They might be different colours, or the purest white."

Lucy's brows, which were constantly dancing about on her

face giving away her every mood, grew still. "Do you get to choose? I'd die for a yellow dress."

"You choose how to behave. Then maybe one day you'll be invited to join those inmost in heaven. They're dressed in radiant light because, like Adam and Eve in Eden, they're innocent."

"You mean they're *naked*?"

Guffaws from Lucy. She stuck out her apron front and shimmied her shoulders in an unchildlike way—mimicking the vaudeville show she'd seen, or so Margaret hoped.

"Don't think of the body that way. Even here your body clothes your spirit. That's what it's for."

Lucy was still snickering, but after a moment her face ironed out. "Your heaven sounds a bloody lot nicer than what those fire-and-brimstone sisters said. Bunch of cows. Bugger them."

What Lucy said next made Margaret quail. "If I can't get out of here, maybe I'll go straight to that angel place."

*

A UNIFORM FINE of $2 in each instance will be imposed on all who, through fault of carelessness, allow any patient for whom they are responsible to escape ...

*

THE MORNING AFTER they'd gathered around Helen's bed, the door opened on that familiar square face. *Attendants will rise promptly when the first signal is given in the morning; unlock the sleeping-room doors; call the patients, and as they*

rise see that beds and bedding are opened for thorough airing,
and so left until after breakfast.

"Up and at 'em, ladies," she clanged.

Still in nightdresses and night braids, bearing chamber pots as though they were sacred vessels, they lined the hall. Elimination was expected before breakfast. Helen, her bowels as yet untrained and her person unused to such intrusions, not to mention the fact that she'd barely eaten, was kept behind, or possibly taken to the infirmary for an enema. Meanwhile, Freda approached Bertha slouching in the queue ahead, and whispered something.

By the time Margaret returned to the room, Bertha was there, her wits clearly restored since dinner the night before. She reclined on her side on Helen's bed, breasts in a sloppy slope under her nightdress, sheenless brown hair loose and matted. Now Margaret could ask if Bertha had seen Lucy in the octagon. But she realized then that she was afraid to know the answer, afraid to hear no. For where would Lucy be if not there?

Bertha pointed to the oblivious Julia. "You? What's your crime?"

Julia went on dressing her hair.

"Imbecile," Bertha pronounced. "This little fright too." She meant the oblivious Rosa. To Freda: "And yourself? What brings you to this rubbish tip?"

When Freda opened her mouth to reply, Bertha recoiled. "Ooo … What happened? They yank out your teeth?"

Freda covered her mouth with her hand.

Margaret she addressed as "Fatty," before launching into her own story.

"Cops picked me up, right? I told them I had connections,

including a certain fellow *very high up* in the political world. They didn't like that. Brought me here. Wait till they see who gets me out!" Her laugh set her breasts jiggling like aspic. "Till then, a change's as good as a rest. I could use one, I guess."

Helen appeared in the doorway. Freda lifted her hand off her mouth and motioned with her chin. Bertha looked over her shoulder.

"Aren't you a little flower?" She got off the bed, smiling. It was horrible. "Hop up, sweetheart." She patted the bed.

Panic inked Helen's pupils.

"This is Bertha," Freda hurried to say. "I asked her to come and meet you. She just wants to help."

"You lie down, honey."

As though sleepwalking, Helen sat on the edge of the bed. She took several steeling breaths before lying back, rigid as a plank.

"I'm going to lift your nightdress. I'm not the first person to do it, eh?"

Bertha's chuckle turned into a long pebbly cough, which immediately broke off when she saw Helen's scar. Her wide face contorted with pity, or disgust. Freda, shocked, glanced at Margaret.

"Okay. I'll have a feel now," Bertha said.

Margaret moved closer, offering her hand to Helen, who accepted it, squeezing, squeezing her whole face while Bertha's fingers kneaded the flesh bowl of her belly. These palpations apparently inconclusive, she instructed Helen to spread her legs.

"Wider. Now bend your knees."

Julia was pinning up her braid, watching with bright-eyed perplexity as Bertha, at the end of the bed, bent close enough that her head disappeared inside the girl's nightdress. She did something with her hand. Tears began coursing down Helen's temples, a good sign, Margaret thought, for you don't squeeze water out of stone.

"Wha-wha-wha she do?" Rosa asked.

At last Bertha emerged, shaking her head. "If a train's ever even pulled into that station, I'm the mayor's wife." At this, she swayed her rump out of the room, adding from the door, "I did fuck 'im. Twice."

*

AFTER LITTLE MORE than a week, Margaret gave up on Lucy's sewing and simply listened to the girl's prattlings. *Endeavour to keep patients from dwelling on their delusions by saying as little to them as possible on the subject, especially never arguing with them about their wrong fancies, as argument only serves to fix their delusions …*

"When I was little, I was as good as those angels of yours. I was! Why are you looking at me like that?"

Here she smacked Margaret on the shoulder. Margaret did no more than frown and look away, stitching on as if Lucy weren't there. This resulted in an immediate apology, something no one else within Margaret's hearing had received.

It seemed quite obvious by then that what would actually help Lucy was to be believed. Wasn't that what Margaret wanted too, not to mention the great majority here? Lucy wanted them to believe that she had a father who cared enough to return for her.

"I *was* good. I did *everything* the sisters asked. But then last year I woke up with the bed all bloody. Nobody told me that was going to happen! And the sisters didn't explain it. One of the other girls who it had already happened to did. That was when I realized they only tell you what they want. So I started saying rubbishy nonsense all the time, just to make them mad."

"Like?"

"Like I seen a bear in the yard, and Mary behind the wash-tubs. Then I ran away for the first time and went to the show I told you about, with the bag-punching sisters. Maybe my father already came to get me. Maybe they told him I was dead. I'd rather be that, dead, than live there anymore with a bunch of liars, which was when I set that fire I told you about."

Pages torn from hymnals, lit with votive candles.

Margaret chided her again about the fire, despite her own distaste for papism. She couldn't help thinking, too, that if Lucy had indeed experienced a shock when her month-lies started, mightn't that have something to do with her behaviour? Margaret herself had suffered much at both ends of that phase of life. Whatever the reason for Lucy's misadventures, her recounting of them so entertained Margaret that she didn't notice until later how her own meditations had fallen by the wayside.

One day the attendant appeared in the doorway. "What do *you* want, ass-face!" Lucy shouted.

The woman did have ample cheeks, reddening now with the insult, like a pair of spanked buttocks. Off she blustered to report to Matron that she'd caught the girl gabbing instead of doing any work—again. Lucy went back on laundry duty with Augusta.

Several weeks after this, while they were getting ready for bed, Lucy confided her nascent plan. She and Augusta had been sent that day to gather soiled towels in the various wcs. Directly above C Ward was D, a men's ward.

"We had to jump over piss puddles. Disgusting! And does that goop even notice? Ow!" She pushed away Margaret's comb.

"You mean Augusta?"

"Yammering at me for the hundredth time h—ow!— she found bits of paper covered in China writing in her husband's pocket. Laundry receipts, I told her, but she won't hear sense. The only way to shut her up is to agree with her. Owww!"

Lucy twisted around to snatch the comb. "I'll do it!" She drew it briskly through her uncooperative curls then plucked a spidery knot from the teeth. This she tossed to the floor before turning her back again so Margaret could braid.

"That was when I noticed the window. The putty round the pane was all broken down. With just my fingernail I scraped it off. One of those thingies was underneath. That buggery little piece that holds the glass in."

"The cleat," said Freda, who was combing her own hair, along with Julia. Rosa was waiting for Margaret.

"If you scrape the putty off, you can open them things easy. The pane'll drop right out." Lucy looked over her shoulder, grinning at Margaret, brows jigging at her own cleverness. "Those floor-pissers'll be kicking themselves they didn't think of it first!"

"You're not going to try climbing out, are you? What if the glass breaks? And it's on the second floor. How will you get down?"

"I'll jump," Lucy declared.

"You can't do that!" She would break in pieces.

"I will. Then I'll go to Vancouver and find my father."

"Honestly, Lucy. How would you ever find him?" Margaret asked.

"I'll go round all the stables. Our name's French. It means 'pretty.' Just how many pretty blacksmiths do you think there are? And, oh. I seen his picture. I got his curls, so I won't get tricked by any no-gooder."

At this she burst into confident guffaws.

"If ever I saw a girl who could look after herself," Freda said to Margaret, "it's the one right in front of you."

*

NO ONE SPOKE of it, yet it happened. *No knives, scissors, razors, stones, or other articles that could be used as weapons, matches, or combustibles, medicine bottles, or poisonous articles, pieces of glass or metal, tools, cords, or ropes are to be permitted on the wards in the reach of patients* … When collecting her mending from the linens room, Margaret added a sheet to the bottom of the basket. Each side scissored, then re-hemmed. No one would notice such a small variation in size. The strips she rolled tightly, to be secreted around the ward. Where? If she hid them in the linens room, Matron might find them during inventory.

In the end, the chosen repository was the obvious one. From bedding the rope would come and there the strips would be tucked, in the cases of the five pillows in the room, eventually to be braided into a sturdy means of escape.

Margaret marvelled. In all her years at the hospital, despite their collective labours, this was the first time those on C Ward had truly worked together. The first time they'd worked for good, instead of simply to run the place. Even Julia helped, her round face glowing with the robust health of northern climes. Her hands, strong as a man's, rolled the strips with a ladylike dexterity, and re-rolled Rosa's when they tumbled, uncoiling, to the floor.

In truth, Margaret was not so much worried about their conspiracy being discovered—let them punish her!—as of it going terribly awry. Lucy might cut herself on the glass, or the rope might break. Or, worst of all, what if Lucy was caught, then used the rope for a fell purpose?

Margaret asked her, "What you said about the other side? That if you couldn't get out of here, you'd go straight to the angels? You didn't mean it, did you? You're going to climb out that window?"

Lucy promised, adding with a saucy laugh, "I might have crossed my toes inside my shoes, mightn't I?"

She would know not to joke about such things if she'd seen what Margaret had seen her first year here.

Before her feet got too bad and she confined herself to her chair by the window, Margaret used to take her turn in the laundry the two days that the women relieved the Chinese. The other male patients worked in the trade shops at carpentry, cobbling, and the like, or the boiler room, or the garden behind the hospital, which was where this incident occurred, with Margaret on her way to the laundry, passing a group of men out turning the rain-sogged soil. One paused in his labour, stabbing the pitchfork in the ground so he could unbutton his canvas coat and cool off. Briefly, he pressed his forearm to his brow. When he looked up, Margaret was herself arrested, for he reminded her of a drawing she'd seen in the New Church tract. An eager seeker gazing skyward while the clouds there parted to reveal that glorious world beyond.

Then, quick as anything, the man flipped the pitchfork round and, bracing the handle on the ground, hurled himself at the tines. Immediately, he collapsed and set to writhing and bleeding in the mud. Too far away to help even if she'd been fit to run, Margaret just stood there, bundle of soiled linens on her hip, scream stuck.

*

HELEN'S FIRST SUNDAY came. *Only the relatives of patients will be allowed to visit them* ... Margaret had seen the mother when Helen was admitted. By the younger woman's honey colouring, or what Margaret glimpsed of it under the broad feather-garden of her hat, Margaret presumed she was the sister. They set off on a promenade of the grounds, the boxy day attendant trundling behind ... *All visitors will be escorted by a hospital employee* ...

The following Sunday they returned and, this time, the sister brought a little boy. He had to be dragged along. Eventually, the party seated themselves on a bench overlooking the river, talking while the boy ran about on the dying lawn.

Sunday was concert day. *The various recreations provided for the use of patients are to be made available to the fullest extent to those who need them. They are an important means for relieving the mind* ... While the orchestra set up, the women pleaded pointlessly with Helen, as they had the previous week. Margaret could tell by their gesticulations. Even from this distance, she could almost read their lips. *You are not pregnant. That is not how it happens. I should have explained it better* ... Or, *Forget about Dugal McBain. He is nothing. Banish him from your heart and mind* ...

As before, when the attendant signalled the end of their half-hour visit, out came their tear-staunching handkerchiefs. The whole time that wraith, Helen, had remained steadfastly silently, hands pressed to her emptiness. They rose from the bench, and Margaret rose too, and went to lie down on her bed.

Ministers of various Christian faiths would soon begin their rounds, clergymen whose versions of the afterlife were either maddeningly vague or appallingly cruel. Their pomposity roused in Margaret the same stabbing urge as Rosa's protruding tongue. Meanwhile, beyond the sealed window, the music started up. She lay listening, giving her eyes a day of rest. Marching tunes and hymns. She moved her lips.

Yes, we'll gather at the river, the beautiful, beautiful river...

Over these weeks, Helen's story had unravelled in night-time whispers. How, when she was clerking in her father's store, she and Dugal McBain would chat before he made his deliveries, which he did by bicycle after school, and Saturdays. He was younger than she, just seventeen, cheerful and jokey, a redhead like Freda, but more carroty.

How, one day, Helen brought him an apple. "Sure you didn't poison it? You got the means to." He swept a hand toward the coloured bottles that filled the shelves, then, taking a bite, clutched his throat and began staggering around the store while Helen laughed and laughed. Her father came out from the back room and gave them both a severe look.

Already, Helen was living for her hours in the store, writing poems to Dugal that she dared not show him.

At Christmas, he turned up sporting a boutonniere. Mistletoe, he claimed, pecking her cheek. "Ow!" she'd cried, because, really, it was holly. Later, undressing for bed, she found three tiny marks above her breast where the holly had pricked her.

Soon she could barely eat. She stopped reading. Dugal was all she thought of. Dugal McBain.

The afternoon it happened, her father had gone down the street for a haircut, leaving Helen alone in the store. When Dugal sauntered in, she seized her chance and confessed her love. He reacted, not with the joyful mutuality she'd dreamed of, but surprise. She could scarcely believe he hadn't guessed, that he hadn't felt the searing waves of ardour streaming off her all those months.

Saying nothing, he took a few steps toward the window— to check for her father, or approaching customers, she realized when he swaggered round the counter. Backing her against it, he forced his sloppy wet tongue inside her mouth.

A long silence followed, Margaret and Freda waiting.

"And?" Freda finally asked.

"I nearly choked."

"That's all he did?"

Helen began to cry again.

"Oh, you poor girl." Margaret sighed.

*

WORD HAD GONE round the wards, probably thanks to Bertha, that Helen was simple. The simple ones, like Rosa, were usually mocked, or shunned. This was another thing that had endeared Lucy to everyone. She stood up for the weakest if they were disparaged within her hearing.

Margaret didn't think Helen was simple. Stubbornly ignorant, perhaps. Too influenced by romantic stories where love climaxes in a kiss and all the drippy business afterward never features on the page. No. She was *innocent*, like the angels inmost in heaven where sexual congress is a spiritual act.

Classed as suicidal, Helen couldn't be left in the care of a fellow patient, especially a crippled one like Margaret. Nor could she work in the kitchen or tailor shop, in reach of knives and scissors. Assigned to the mop brigade, she silently swabbed the common spaces. During meals, she ate under the attendant's watch, taking a gulp of water between bites to get each one swallowed, a torture that precluded conversation.

Conversation happened only by night.

"I saw your scar," Freda whispered.

"They did that to me at the sanitorium."

"Did they tell you what it was for?"

"To make me feel better."

Margaret asked, "Did you?"

"No. It hurt a lot. And Papa was furious that they did it. He said it cost eighteen dollars a week for me to stay there and all they did was ruin my future. He says no one will marry me now."

Freda heaved a sigh. "You understand then that you can't have a baby."

"I'm having Dugal's baby. I love him."

Margaret pictured the frantic gesticulations of mother and sister as they too tried to bring Helen to her senses. Then something Lucy had said about Augusta came to mind: that the only way to shut her up was to agree with her. Though blurted in frustration, which was more or less Lucy's permanent roiling state, she was right. The struggle to protect one's truth—not convince others of it, but keep it safe from their unremitting disbelief—is so overwhelming and exhausting that when offered the respite of even *feigned* agreement, an immense calm descends, reassuring and vindicating.

"And after you have the baby?" Margaret asked, as she should have before. "Will you marry Dugal?"

"Papa sent him packing. I'd go home, if they'll take me back. They're ashamed of me, you see."

Freda picked up Margaret's line of questioning. "And what about the baby?"

"Oh! I couldn't bring it!"

"There was a girl here recently," Margaret said. "She was raised in an orphanage."

"I expected that would happen." Helen rolled over so her narrow back faced Margaret. For some time, she quietly cried.

"When will you have the baby?" Freda asked.

"November," Helen replied, adding, as though to show she did know her facts, "it takes nine months."

"But often they come early," Margaret chirped. "Wouldn't that be a blessing?"

*

WHEN MARGARET FIRST read the New Church tract, she'd been surprised to learn that angels possessed mouths and tongues and ears just as people did, and that they spoke in a language differentiated into words. She'd expected them to communicate mind to mind. Why, on C Ward they frequently read each other's thoughts, as when they'd silently agreed to help Lucy.

As when Margaret made the painful trip to the tailoring

shop where Freda worked cutting the pattern pieces. Freda pulled from her apron front a handful of scraps, which she added to Margaret's basket. At luncheon, she brought two buttons, surreptitiously dropped in Margaret's lap.

Unlike a rope, a rag baby could be passed off as a seamstress's fancy, so Margaret hid it in plain view, in her basket— limbs, body, and head detached, unstuffed until the night of its birth. Half the size of a flesh baby, lumpy and criss-crossed with seams, its only features were two flat bone buttons for eyes.

Studying it, Freda said, "She'd have to be insane to believe she gave birth to this."

"Maybe Dugal McBain didn't have a nose."

Rare for Freda to laugh. She did now.

Late that night, Freda woke Helen with glad tidings. "Look what's come." She drew back the covers to show the rag baby she'd slipped in with Helen while she slept.

Helen sat up and stared at it.

"You have to feed it now. I'll show you."

Freda settled beside Helen. She opened her own nightdress and pressed the doll to her breast, the sorrowful droop of which Margaret could just make out in the dark.

"I had a baby just like this," said Freda, who spoke of herself even less than she laughed. "Actually, I had five. But the last one—he'd be almost three now. He gave me some trouble. Always hungry, always screaming for the breast. I had nothing for him."

"Why?" Helen asked.

"Because you have to eat yourself to suckle a baby. You've got to start eating now too, Helen. I've seen you in the dining room."

"Why didn't you eat?"

"The cupboard was empty, my purse too. And there were four other mouths to feed first."

"Aren't you married?"

"Sure. But if I dared mentioned it when he got home, he'd get busy knocking the lights out of me. Now take your baby and show me you can do it."

Margaret watched as Helen accepted the baby from Freda. With reluctance, she opened the front of her nightdress, exposing one inverted teacup.

"It may not latch at first," Freda explained. "It may cry. And you might lose your mind a bit, especially with the lack of sleep. But you won't, will you?"

"What?" Helen asked, staring down at the doll with bleary incomprehension.

"Lose your mind," Freda said.

From her bed, Margaret said, "In a few days, we'll give it to the orphanage. You needn't think about it again. You'll get well and go home."

All at once Helen seemed to wake up. "But I didn't have it. My sister said it's the worst pain ever. Like being torn in two. I didn't feel anything."

She thrust the doll back at Freda who, with a glance at Margaret, sighed and returned to her bed, slippers slapping in defeat. Margaret lay down again herself. None of them slept, except Rosa and poor drugged Julia, both of whom had missed this hushed and frustrating scene.

The next day Rosa awoke to monthly troubles, reminding Margaret of Lucy. She was put in the bath while the others went about the morning routine, then allowed to lie abed, moaning. Feeling sorry for her, Margaret stupidly offered her the surrogate to cuddle.

Now here *was* a simpleton! In the days that followed, Rosa wouldn't stop asking for the dolly. Several times she snuck it from the basket and, when discovered, backed into the corner with her tongue out, denying she'd ever touched it.

"What are you holding behind you then?" Margaret asked her. Sniffling, Rosa returned the baby. Margaret told her, "I'll cut it to pieces. Would you like that?"

So harsh! Rosa began to cry and her tears reminded Margaret of her purpose. "I'm sorry. I would never do that."

Or so she thought at the time.

*

IT IS THE wish of those in charge of the Hospital that all may be free in their social enjoyments and as little restricted in their conduct as good order and self-respect will permit. Any reasonable amount of "fun" will not be objected to …

Labour Day carried no hint of autumn. The lawn had, by then, reversely transfigured from emerald expanse to burnt brown field. But there were other things for the public to admire when the grounds opened for the annual picnic—the elegant stone buildings, the beautiful river rolling along, the food and entertainment. The orchestra would play, incidentally, and for the parade. All week Margaret had watched through the window the patients rehearsing their forced march.

Now the others were in the kitchen preparing the picnic luncheon. Sandwich triangles of cucumber or potted meat. Potato salad, beetroot salad. Tomato aspic. An assortment of cakes and squares. Lemonade or tea. Margaret sat in her usual spot, remembering last night's dream.

She'd gone to heaven, apparently by streetcar, for through its window she watched the goings on. Citizens flitted busily in and out of buildings that seemed constructed out of colourful wooden blocks, many decorated with filigreed spires and eaves, and impossible icing-like intricacies. Everywhere ladders disappeared into the clouds. No one had a face, just a patch of light, like sun glinting off metal. Meanwhile, the streetcar glided soundlessly along. No grating wheels on rails, no bell ringing the stops. It might have been floating on air. And across the aisle sat the New Church woman. But how had Margaret recognized her without a face? By dream logic, she supposed, which might be the same unstable logic that had landed her here in the hospital.

The car stopped. The woman nodded, directing Margaret's attention to the front. And there stood a sturdy figure in a yellow dress waiting to disembark.

"Margaret?" she heard.

Let it not be her, Margaret was praying, *please. Let it not be her…*

"Margaret?"

She looked up and saw Matron Fillmore hovering in the doorway.

"I have good news," Matron said, and these words seemed to be an answer to Margaret's prayer.

Swelling with hope, she asked, "About Lucy?"

Briefly, the hawk face crimped. "No. You've been chosen as a hospital honouree, Margaret. The superintendent is going to present your ribbon at the picnic. What do you think of that?" She produced a thin version of a smile.

"Just tell me if she's in the octagon. That's all I want to know."

Matron's mouth retracted to its official place. "Don't be

so pigheaded, Margaret. You know I can't talk about other patients."

A police car had brought Lucy back the very next day at dawn. The whole hospital heard her screeches, louder than any siren. Margaret hadn't been quick enough to the window, but Freda saw her, bound up in a restraining camisole, borne into the hospital over a blue serge shoulder, the way the butcher delivered a cured pig to the kitchen. It was the last anyone had heard or seen of that blazing comet of a girl, until she appeared last night in Margaret's dream.

Tears came. "Can't you at least tell me that she's come to no harm?"

Matron's Maritime vowels swam toward Margaret's ears. "Will you attend the celebration? You deserve that ribbon, Margaret. No one here works as hard as you. And, you know, it occurred to me today that you haven't been outside for a very long time. Wouldn't you like to go?"

If she'd been surer on her feet, she would have lunged at Matron with her needle.

"I would not."

Matron turned and left. Then Margaret was alone again, trying to blink away that girl in yellow, alive on the other side. *Love, be useful, love, be useful, love.*

She could not.

But several hours later, watching the grounds fill with shell-shocked relatives and the luridly curious, Margaret changed her mind. Those in Lawn House, closest to the isolation annex, had nothing to report on Lucy. But that didn't mean she wasn't there. With all these visitors, surely no one would bother about beribboned Margaret limping off to see if a freckled smirk would show itself in a window. And it was true that she hadn't been outside, not for years. She would go.

She'd barely got halfway down the hall when the first blats of the tuba sounded. Ahead, Rosa came backing out of the WC. She was supposed to be mustering for the parade, but seeing Margaret, she flew to her.

The doll again! Breathless, tugging Margaret's sleeve, Rosa kept trying to spit out the word. "Daw-daw. Daw..." She pointed toward the WC.

"You get back outside now or they'll punish you." Margaret shooed her, but Rosa wouldn't budge.

"Daw!" Then came a rare, perfectly enunciated word. "Bum!"

"I'll go," she assured the panting girl, who turned and ran.

The door to the WC stood ajar. Margaret hobbled in. There, at the end of the row of sinks, crouched Helen, on whom Margaret had more or less given up. Head bowed, she didn't notice Margaret swaying in the doorway, confused and staring. From the girl's animal grunts and whimpers, it sounded as though she was moving her bowels on the floor. Some did this, from spite or incontinence. Margaret would never have expected filth from Helen.

She noticed then that both the girl's hands were working something under her skirt. Beside her lay a pair of cast-off drawers.

From outside—*pah-boom, pah-boom, pah-boom*. Helen glanced up and, seeing Margaret, scrambled to a stand. With a panicked look, she said, "I have to have it. I have to."

How terrier-like, the way the human mind clamped upon its notions. How singular and strange. Outrageous, tragic. Lunatic, other minds said. Why Helen's had fixed itself this way, Margaret didn't know any more than she knew why

Augusta's fixed on Chinamen, or Bertha believed herself politically well-connected, or Lucy that her father would come for her. Perhaps there was another side to Helen's story. Perhaps she'd accused Dugal, falsely, and her conscience needed it to be true. Or maybe it was just a story from a book. In any event, if Margaret could find the words or means to satisfy Helen's mind, it might release its grip. If not, Helen would soon be discovered here trying to achieve the impossible—to stuff a baby inside herself. And then what would happen to her?

She tried not to alarm her. "Can I see, Helen?"

Helen slowly raised her skirt, revealing the rag baby hanging by its arm. Somehow she'd got it lodged that far inside her.

Gently, Margaret tutted. She asked to deliver Helen of the baby, hoping it would satisfy her to have it pulled from between her legs. "It's almost out now. One last push."

Helen shook her head. Her mouth opened to scream.

"Don't," Margaret told her.

Though it was forbidden to carry scissors, Margaret almost always had a pair at hand, either on the sill or in her apron pocket. She fished them out and, like a midwife with a cord to sever, showed them to Helen.

"What are you going to do?" Helen asked.

A finger to her lips, Margaret moved closer. "It won't hurt. You'll see."

She cupped her hand to catch it so it wouldn't fall to the floor. Snip! The infant's foot dropped into her palm. Margaret held it out to Helen, who had, after all, conceived through her mouth.

She reached for the faucet, turned it on. A little water to help the swallowing.

*

15 January 1909
The Provincial Hospital for the Insane
New Westminster, B.C.

Dear Mr H.,

In reply to your letter dated 28 November 1908, I beg to tell
you that I was very much surprised—not by your daughter's
claim of mistreatment, but that you apparently put some
credence in it. Discerning truth from fabrication is one of
the signifiers of a sound mind.

I beg also to remind you that Helen was admitted to
this hospital in a suicidal state after a failure of treatment
by another institution. From the outset she manifested a
desire for self-starvation, and though she could be cajoled
into eating during the early weeks of her stay, eventually a
restraining chair and spoon-feeding proved necessary. Bruis-
ing is the inevitable result of these interventions. As to her
medical emergency, I assure you that, in addition to alien-
ists, numerous physicians are in employ. Helen's condition
presented as constipation and for it she was given the usual
treatment of enemas and castor oil.

Your daughter's insanity is inherited, Mr H. It is there-
fore not the fault of this institution that she somehow managed to consume such a quantity of cloth. (We suspect she
ate her underdrawers, as those were the only article missing,
and that is the reason you have received the extra charge of
$6.) We suspect this was done to replicate the abdominal
swelling that would have accompanied pregnancy, which
our physician reasonably diagnosed as gas, and the pain of
labour resulting from the subsequent blockage. That she

managed to accomplish this whilst under near-continuous restraint boggles the mind. She is nothing if not determinedly devious.

One role of this institution, Mr H., is to replace the psychotic family with a morally controlled environment conducive to mental health. I extend an invitation to you to visit here and disabuse yourself of these malicious claims.

Sincerely,
Dr C. Doherty, Superintendent

*

IN THE NEW year Margaret began each day by greeting sleep-addled Julia in her own singsong. "Heeva huamenta, Julia!"

Margaret's mouth and tongue formed the sounds that, reaching Julia's ear, prompted so beautiful a bleary smile. Seeing it, Margaret's purpose, badly tested of late, was reaffirmed.

Since then, Julia had been teaching other words to Margaret, who now sat muttering as she worked. "Omella, omella, omella ..." Only by continuous repetition could she fix this gibber to memory—no easy feat for a woman of her age. If she understood correctly, it meant "stitch," or perhaps "sew."

"Omella, omella, omella..."

"Margaret?"

Matron was in the doorway.

"The superintendent would like to speak with you."

Though her heart lurched, Margaret calmly set her unfinished work in her basket. She'd wondered when she would be called to account for Helen, whom she prayed for every night along with Lucy. God would call her to account on the other side as well, but she was much less afraid of God. He wouldn't punish her; the superintendent might. But then again, if he did, if she found herself in the octagon—the only possibility since she never partook in any other privilege they might punitively withhold, no concerts, visits, or airings—wouldn't that bring her closer to Lucy, if not in body, then in spirit?

"Do you want to take my arm, Margaret?" Matron asked.

"I do not."

She focused on her feet dragging along in their side-slit slippers. Lately, a blurriness had settled on her eyes so that she'd had to request a mechanical threader. Worry was to blame. But now, perhaps, the superintendent would tell her what had happened after the medics carried Helen off, screaming, the way she'd screamed when she first arrived. Piece by piece, with Margaret's help, Helen had got herself with child. And then came the inevitable agony that Helen believed was a woman's due. Lucy's mother had died in childbirth. So many did.

They reached the administration wing. Dr Doherty's office door was open. As Margaret shuffled nearer, he came into view, waiting for her behind the dark wood bastion of his desk, a doughy man with a cleaved chin whose head seemed precariously perched on his high, stiff collars. She'd spoken to him only once before, when she'd been admitted, having forfeited the opportunity at the Labour Day picnic. Now he watched her slow progress with an affected blankness, giving no clue at all as to her fate.

When she crossed the threshold, he politely rose. Only then did Margaret realize he wasn't alone for, slumped in a chair off to the side, was Lloyd dressed up in town clothes—collarless shirtsleeves and suspenders, jacket and hat piled in his lap. At the sight of his potato nose and shrewd eyes, a word popped into her head. *Ass-face.* Apart from the stained fringe under the potato, he looked the same.

"Hullo, Mags," he said, not bothering to stand. "You've got nice and fat."

She turned quickly away from him and, accepting the chair Dr Doherty gestured to, took pains to pull it the maximum distance from Lloyd before plunking herself down.

"Mrs Cox," the doctor said. "How are you?"

He was enveloped in blur. There was a rushing in her ears too, which dizzied her. She gripped the chair's arms so that she might stay in it if she fainted, for, though she was loathe to have Lloyd's eyes anywhere on her, she especially didn't want them on her backside.

Briefly, the doctor consulted the papers before him. "You were admitted in 1903 suffering from religious excitement and delusions."

Margaret had no recollection of what she'd croaked out back then. She was sure, though, that she hadn't mentioned the woman on the streetcar, or how she'd got off and followed her. Margaret had been so low then. She'd quarrelled with all her neighbours, hadn't a friend in the world. Now she knew that boredom and spite were a dark cloth she'd thrown over her own life, a shroud in fact. Yet the woman on the streetcar had practically glowed. Just think if Margaret had stayed in her seat! She'd have done away with herself and gone to Hell where she'd be dressed in filthy rags. Instead, here she was, living for that kind, ordered existence that waited on the other side, where she'd be dressed by God Himself.

"How it happened," Lloyd piped up, "was I come back from three months in camp and she won't get out of bed. Just lies there muttering about wanting to die. The doctor said it was the change of life. Gave her the Pinkham's Compound." Lloyd laughed. "'An irritable woman is a source of misery not only to herself.' Right, Mags?"

Dr Doherty shuffled the papers. "This was Dr Twombly who signed her committal paper?"

Margaret sensed Lloyd nodding. "Pinkham's didn't help," he said, and cleared his throat, making that porridgy sound she hated.

"No medicine can cure your wife of an inherited condition," Dr Doherty told him. "At this institution we aim to reduce the symptoms of inflicted persons so they might return to normal life."

"She's worked very hard here," Matron interjected. She was standing by the door, hands folded in front of her apron, lips still compressed. She almost sounded sad.

"Mrs Cox?" Dr Doherty asked. "Do you still think that you're an angel?"

Margaret startled. "I never did say that. I said that if I behaved like one whilst here among the living, when my soul undresses of my body, they will welcome me."

"Into their little houses and whatnot?"

"Yes."

Lloyd laughed. "I don't care what she talks about. I need her back at home. Look here, Mags." He leaned over and flicked her shoulder. She nearly jumped out of her skin. "I went and got my arm crushed. Look at it."

He lifted the clothes out of his lap. She would not look.

"I can't do for myself like this. I need you to come home now. You can talk all the nonsense you want. I just won't listen."

"This will be a six-month probationary discharge, Mr Cox," Dr Doherty said.

"I don't know what that is, but I won't let her bother me."

Matron could just be heard under the roar in Margaret's ears. "We will certainly miss you, Margaret, and welcome you back to visit any time."

With considerable help from the arms of the chair, Margaret wordlessly rose. She left with Matron who, after closing the office door, told her to go ahead to her room.

"Wait," Matron said before Margaret had even turned. Under the stiff cap, her face softened. "This is all so sudden. I didn't know until this morning that you'd be discharged. I would have got you a little gift. You've been such a help to me. Such a help."

For a moment they just stood there, Margaret's feet throbbing. Matron's pebble eyes darted about, as though she had something to add. *The names and particulars of the conduct of any of those suffering from insanity must not be made subjects of gossip outside the institution...*

"Because I can trust you, I will tell you that Lucy's misadventure had a happy outcome."

Seemingly on its own, Margaret's hand reached out and clutched Matron's sleeve. Matron removed it and, with unexpected tenderness, held it between her own.

"Her little outing made the *Daily*. We are never pleased with that sort of publicity! However...Despite not mentioning Lucy by name, it did say that she'd come here from the convent. The next thing you know a letter arrived."

"From her father?"

"Her stepmother. She has half-sisters too. She's behaving herself with them, by all accounts. You look like you found a diamond in your soup, Margaret." Here Matron actually smiled. "Carry on. I'll find you some clothes to travel in."

Matron brisked off, leaving Margaret in the empty corridor, vibrating with joy.

But, oh. There was Lloyd. Could she run like Lucy? Hardly. Ahead, through the glass in the double front doors, Margaret saw that it was airing period. The rain must have finally stopped. At least she could tell someone that she was leaving and spare them the pain of not knowing where she'd gone.

She shuffled along and, reaching the door, pushed it—so heavy! And then the shock, not just the cold of the air, but after years of sealed rooms, the barrage of odours. The fishy river, the green scent of firs, the wet black loam. Lucy had called the hospital a stink hole, but when you live in it, you don't notice sweat or farts or the emanations from two hundred chamber pots. Likewise, you sometimes don't see what's before your own eyes, for out on the lawn, restored to the verdancy of winter, the patients moved about in their male and female groupings, dressed in identical garb. Cloaks of grey serge covered dresses and trousers alike, darker at the hem where the rain on the grass had wicked up. Wings were just a fancy for the birds, which she saw too, flitting in the trees. She heard their singing and, dizzy again, had to steady herself against the jamb.

Her eye searched for someone from her room, Freda preferably. But then it lit upon the river. Silvery, cloud-cast, it never ceased, which meant it was eternal. Shall we gather at the river, the beautiful river, where bright angel feet have trod?

At last the blur lifted off someone she recognized. Julia with her braided halo. Yes, we'll gather at the river, this beautiful river flowing by.

A male attendant cried out, "Back to work, lads, lassies! Back to work!"

*

HOSPITAL FOR INSANE ACT
Form B (Section 7 (b).)

MEDICAL CERTIFICATE

I, the undersigned, . . . Dr C. Doherty . . . Do hereby declare and certify that—

I have with care and diligence personally observed and examined within seven days prior to the date of this Certificate, namely, on the . . . *30* . . . day of . . . *January, 1909* . . . *Margaret C.* . . . , and as a result of such examinations find the said . . . *Margaret C.* . . . is insane and a proper person for care and treatment in some Hospital or Institution for the Insane, as an insane person under the provisions of the Statute.

I have formed the above opinion upon the subjoined facts, viz.: —

(a.) Facts indicating insanity personally observed by me as follows: —

The patient said . . . *she was in heaven among the angels and was innocent of having done something to result in her removal.*

The patient did . . . *Considered a suitable candidate for a provisional discharge, she made no objection to this arrangement, but subsequent to the interview disappeared from her room. Several hours later, she was located hiding on the grounds.*

The patient's appearance was . . . *unclothed.*

The patient's manner was . . . *belligerent.*

Other facts indicating insanity as communicated to me by others . . . *See attached notes from original admittance for dementia praecox excited by Swedenborgian theology. Matron Fillmore reports that during her time here, approximately five years, the patient made excellent progress, working diligently for the tailoring shop, albeit independently due to lameness. While considered chronic, her false beliefs had quieted.*

The answers to these questions contained in this statement are to the best of my knowledge, information, and belief.

Signed . . . *Dr C. Doherty*
P.O. address . . . *New Westminster*

ACKNOWLEDGEMENTS

ALL THE STORIES in this collection owe a debt in some way to previously existing works. Some are directly referenced, others alluded to, or hidden in the text. I would like to acknowledge these creators here: Robert Burns, Luis Buñuel, Anton Chekhov, Emily Dickinson, and T. S. Eliot. The wording of Ketman's epiphany in his colon in "The Procedure" was strongly influenced by an 1866 article by E. B. Tylor in *Fortnightly Review*, as quoted in Robert Wright's *The Evolution of God*, Back Bay Books, 2009. "Homing" was inspired by Susan Orlean's article, "Little Wing," published in the *New Yorker* in 2006; additionally, Akberet Seyoum Beyene's writing and friendship educated me about Eritrea. The surely true article "Shocked Russian surgeons open man who thought he had a tumour . . . to find a FIR TREE inside his lung," by Will Stewart for *Mailonline*, 2016, led me to write "Yolki-Palki." Three articles by Dr M. E. Kelm were the starting point for

"From the Archives of the Hospital for the Insane": "A Life Apart: The Experience of Women and the Asylum Practice of Charles Doherty at British Columbia's Provincial Hospital from the Insane, 1905–1915," published in BCHM, volume 11:1994; "Women, Families and the Provincial Hospital for the Insane, British Columbia, 1905–1915," published in *Journal of Family History* volume 19, number 2, 1994; and "'The only place likely to do her any good': The Admission of Women to British Columbia's Provincial Hospital from the Insane," published in *BC Studies*, number 96, Winter 1992–93. I furthermore borrowed liberally from original materials I sourced from the BC Archives. Patient numbers and some names were changed to protect the identity of actual people, all of whom have been fictionalized.

Tatiana Tyuleneva helped me translate the epigraph of this book from the original Russian. Harry Killas gave me the idea for "Charity." Marina Endicott, Paul Headrick, Shaena Lambert, Kathy Page, and Morna McLeod generously provided critical feedback and moral support over many drafts. These stories would be paler versions of themselves without this input. Thank you, dear friends.

Versions of the following stories were previously published: "The Procedure" in *The Walrus*, March/April 2022; "All Our Auld Acquaintances Are Gone" in *Canadian Notes and Queries*, number 109, Spring/Summer 2021, and reprinted in *Best Canadian Stories* 2023, Biblioasis, 2022; "Obscure Objects" in *The New Quarterly* 90, 2004, and reprinted in *Found Press Quarterly*, Summer 2011, and the *2016 Short Story Advent Calendar*, Hingston and Olsen Publishing, 2016. I am grateful to the editors of these publications.

Likewise, words cannot adequately express my appreciation for Jackie Kaiser, my agent; John Metcalf and Dan Wells, who edited this collection; and my husband, Bruce Sweeney.

I am also profoundly grateful for the financial support of the Canada Council for the Arts and the BC Arts Council during the writing of this book.

CAROLINE ADDERSON is the author of five novels (*A Russian Sister, Ellen in Pieces, The Sky Is Falling, Sitting Practice,* and *A History of Forgetting*), two previous collections of short stories (*Pleased to Meet You* and *Bad Imaginings*), as well as many books for young readers. Her award nominations include the *Sunday Times* EFG Private Bank Short Story Award, the International IMPAC Dublin Literary Award, two Commonwealth Writers' Prizes, the Governor General's Literary Award, the Rogers' Trust Fiction Prize, and the Scotiabank Giller Prize longlist. The recipient of three BC Book Prizes, three CBC Literary Awards, and the Marian Engel Award for mid-career achievement, Caroline lives and writes in Vancouver.